Flynn Rawley's Picture?"

The old messenger jumped violently as he turned to look through the doorway into her bedroom.

Toni followed his gaze as his voice rose in puritan outrage. "Are you his fancy piece? 'Cos I don't hold with goings-on."

"No, I'm not his 'fancy piece,'" Toni said, looking at him curiously. "I'm his ex-wife."

"Aha! But you kept his picture. You're still spoony on him, ain't you?"

"I am certainly *not*. On the contrary, I think leaving him was the best day's work I ever did. That man is a thoroughly unscrupulous fraud, and I've only just realized how low he can sink."

As she spoke, she moved determinedly toward him, and he edged away frantically. "What you doin'? Keep your hands off me, you brazen hussy—ow!"

Toni seized his moustache and wrenched it off in one piece. She stood there, holding her trophy triumphantly while her victim rubbed his upper lip.

"You ought to be shot, Flynn Rawley."

Dear Reader,

Welcome to Silhouette! Our goal is to give you hours of unbeatable reading pleasure, and we hope you'll enjoy each month's six new Silhouette Desires. These sensual, provocative love stories are both believable and compelling—sometimes they're poignant, sometimes humorous, but always enjoyable.

Indulge yourself. Experience all the passion and excitement of falling in love along with our heroine as she meets the irresistible man of her dreams and together they overcome all obstacles in the path to a happy ending.

If this is your first Desire, I hope it'll be the first of many. If you're already a Silhouette Desire reader, thanks for your support! Look for some of your favorite authors in the coming months: Stephanie James, Diana Palmer, Dixie Browning, Ann Major and Doreen Owens Malek, to name just a few.

Happy reading!

Isabel Swift
Senior Editor

SDRL-7/85

LUCY GORDON

Just Good Friends

Silhouette Desire
Published by Silhouette Books New York
America's Publisher of Contemporary Romance

SILHOUETTE BOOKS
300 East 42nd St., New York, N.Y. 10017

ISBN: 0-373-05363-0

First Silhouette Books printing July 1987

America's Publisher of Contemporary Romance

Printed in the U.S.A.

Books by Lucy Gordon

Silhouette Romance

The Carrister Pride #306
Island of Dreams #353
Virtue and Vice #390
Once Upon a Time #420
A Pearl Beyond Price #503

Silhouette Special Edition

Legacy of Fire #148
Enchantment in Venice #185

Silhouette Desire

Take All Myself #164
The Judgment of Paris #179
A Coldhearted Man #245
My Only Love, My Only Hate #317
A Fragile Beauty #333
Just Good Friends #363

LUCY GORDON

is English but lives in Venice, Italy, and is married to a Venetian. They met in Venice, fell in love the first evening and got engaged two days later. After fifteen years they're still happily married. For twelve years Lucy was a writer on an English women's magazine. She interviewed many of the world's most interesting men including Warren Beatty, Richard Chamberlain, Roger Moore, Sir Alec Guinness and Sir John Gielgud. She also has camped out with lions in Africa and has had many other unusual experiences, which at times provide the backgrounds to her books.

One

The telephone by the bed rang ten times before it raised any sign of life. On the eleventh ring a hand appeared from under the flowered quilt, groped vaguely in the direction of the phone, located it, grasped the receiver and fell back onto the pillow as though exhausted. A man's voice came from the earpiece, "Hello—hello, Toni, are you there? *Toni?*"

Slowly the hand retreated under the quilt, taking the receiver with it. "Mmm?"

"Toni?"

"Mmm."

"Are you still there?"

"Mmm."

"Are you awake?"

"Just about."

"Alive?"

"Problematic."

"Well, wake up, I want to talk to you."

"Shepherd Dunway, what do you mean by phoning me at this hour?"

"It's four in the afternoon."

"It is?"

The quilt stirred. A head of flaming-red hair, cut short, appeared as far as the eyes, which swiveled to the bedside clock. "Oh, heck, yes it is," muttered Antonia Locksley. She struggled farther up in the bed and tried to gather her wits. "Hello Shep."

"It must have been quite a party."

"It was. We waited up for the early editions of the papers."

"And I'll bet the champagne flowed when you saw your reviews."

"Mmm." She was momentarily submerged in happy memories. "It flowed like water. It tasted a bit like water, too, as a matter of fact. It probably *was* water. I didn't care. After I read those reviews the whole world was made of champagne."

"'But the real triumph of the evening was the direction by Toni Locksley,'" Shep quoted. "'For once the director was the star.' 'Toni Locksley has that magic touch...' You see, I know them all by heart."

"Not half as well as I do," she assured him.

She was awake now, blissfully reliving the night before, when *Dead and Alive*, a new play, had opened in London to the unmistakable sound of success. Toni had been called onstage and greeted by a cheer that still echoed in her memory.

She had been directing plays for four years. She'd served her apprenticeship in the sticks and a year ago Shep Dunway's production company had offered her a chance in one of the more notable provincial theaters. She'd created a success and Shep had promptly given her more work. This time she'd done so well that another company had offered her *Dead and Alive* in London. It was a minor theater on the outskirts of the city, far from the bright lights of the West End, but the critics from the national papers had been there for opening night. When their reviews had appeared in the early hours, there was no doubt that Toni was on her way.

After doing two plays under Shep's aegis she'd felt a deep satisfaction at emerging to stand on her own feet. But he was a dear friend, and her moment of triumph had held one disappointment: "I wish you could have been there last night."

"You can't regret it more than I do," he said in his gruff, kindly voice. "I meant to come, but Mel had a heart attack."

"Oh, no! Is he...?"

"He's alive and I think he'll stay that way."

"I hope so. I'm very fond of Mel. He taught me a lot." Mel was also a director and had been largely responsible for bringing Toni to Shep's attention a year ago.

"The thing is," Shep was saying, "it leaves me in a bit of a spot. He was due to start work on a new show in a couple of weeks and I've got to replace him urgently. Of course I know you're supposed to be booked for something else soon, but I've heard rumors that that might be falling through." Shep stopped hopefully.

"They're more than rumors," Toni said wryly. "The leading actor had director approval, and he asked for some preliminary discussion. He came to my apartment that evening and the things he tried to 'discuss' weren't in the script—not for the director, anyway. I told him to forget it and he sneered and said that if he was going to put up with being bossed around by a woman there had to be compensations. That's when he lunged at me."

Shep chuckled. "Hadn't anyone warned him that you'd taken judo lessons?"

"Well, he knows now if he didn't then."

"I heard you broke his arm."

"It's a lie," she said indignantly. "He got nothing worse than a sprained wrist, and he got that falling off the sofa. He went screaming back to the producer and said nothing would persuade him to work with 'that evil harpy.' At any rate the contract was never finalized."

"Your words are music to my ears. So you're free then?"

"That's right. But look, Shep, I don't *need* a job. You don't have to—"

Shep's groan reached her down the line. "Toni, will you stop being so prickly? This isn't charity. You're a brilliant young director who can pick and choose. I'm begging for crumbs from *your* table, not the other way around. Keep telling yourself that."

Toni chuckled. She was ferociously independent by nature, and some people found her attitude alarming. But Shep had always laughed at her until she relaxed. "All right, I'll believe it," she said. "What was Mel starting on?"

"*The Merry War*. You must have heard of it. It's going to be a musical version of Shakespeare's *Much Ado About Nothing*, concentrating on the Beatrice and Benedick story, and with some very good songs. Toni . . . are you there?"

Toni eased herself from the daze that his words had begun to wrap around her. "Yes, Shep, I'm here, and I'm sorry, I can't do it. It's very nice of you to think of me, but it's out of the question."

"Now why would that be?" Shep asked persuasively, despite the fact that he already knew the answer and had been anticipating this reaction all along.

"I've never done a musical before. It's a specialized art."

"You'll have George Alladale as assistant director. He's very experienced on the music side."

"Then why not let him do the whole thing?"

"Because there's more to directing a musical than staging song-and-dance sequences. It all has to be properly integrated, and that means having a good dramatic director in overall control. You're the one I want."

"Shep, I'm sorry, but it's quite impossible."

There was a silence. Then Shep sighed, "You're a coward, Toni Locksley. I'm ashamed of you."

"Now, wait a minute—"

"All this stuff you've been handing me is nothing but excuses," Shep went on as if she hadn't spoken. "You know, and I know, that the real reason you're backing off this project is that the star is going to be Flynn Rawley."

"Well, can you blame me?" she asked indignantly. "Flynn Rawley is the most harebrained, irresponsible..." Words failed her.

"He also happens to be a great star with enough charisma to set the theater alight just by standing on the stage, never mind acting."

"Shep, I'm telling you that *no* director who wanted to retain her sanity would ever work with that madman. He's crazy himself and has a disruptive influence on the rest of the cast. You won't get any work out of the chorus girls because they'll all be swooning over him."

"It's not his fault they fall in love with him," Shep said mildly. "Nature made him that way."

"And doesn't he know it!"

"Ah now, be fair. No one could call Flynn vain. It's incredible, considering what he's got going for him, but he isn't."

"All right," Toni allowed in a large-minded spirit. "I'll grant you that, *for an actor*, he isn't vain."

"And even if he was, it wouldn't make any difference to you as his director. All you need care about is the performance you can get out of him."

"Performance! Hah! Do you know he plays practical jokes? I've seen him reduce an entire rehearsal to chaos simply by going through his role with a funny walk. The director nearly shot himself. What's more—" Toni produced her trump card "—he'll never agree to be directed by a woman. You just try putting this idea to him—"

"I have. He loved it."

There was a silence. "What did you say?" Toni asked eventually.

"Flynn's all for you being the director. He can't wait to get started. He wants you to know—" Shep assumed a mechanical, reciting tone "—that he has the deepest admiration and respect for your abilities, and he's sure that together the two of you can create a really wonderful show."

"Eyewash!"

"Well, that's what he asked me to say," Shep said, resuming his normal voice.

"It's another of his practical jokes. I can't possibly work with him."

"Toni, I don't know what's gotten into you. I thought you told me your marriage ended amicably."

"It did. And anyway, it was four years ago. Flynn and I don't see each other often, but when we do we're the best of friends. When he's on location for a film we exchange funny postcards. I send him messages on his opening nights and he sends me messages on mine. It's all unbelievably civilized.

"He's a nice man. I'll even go further; he's a warm, witty, wonderful human being and the fact that he was a totally lousy husband was probably my fault in some way."

"That's what he says, too."

"That it was *my* fault?"

"No, that he was a lousy husband. But I don't want you to remarry him, I want you to direct him in a play." Shep assumed a wheedling voice, "This is going to be the big one, Toni. If you miss it, you'll kick yourself."

"If I take it I'll kick myself."

"Look, don't make a decision yet—"

"Shep, you're not hearing me. I've made my decision and the answer's no."

"I'm really disappointed in you, Toni. I'm not a man to say things like 'After all I've done for you,' but I thought we were friends."

She ground her teeth. "Shep, that's hitting below the belt."

"Of course, my dear. That's where it's most effective. Look, just read the script. That's all I ask."

Toni hesitated. All her professional instincts were urging her to accept. This was her first West End chance, the kind of offer aspiring directors dreamed about—a big show that would have the public's attention from the start because the leading man was the charismatic Flynn Rawley. For anyone else that would have been the clincher. For Toni, it was the problem.

"All right, I'll read it," she said. "But only on the understanding that I'm not committed."

"Fine. I'll have a copy to you in an hour." Shep hung up.

Toni jumped out of bed and flung off her nightgown. She plunged into a cold shower and felt her flesh tingle delightfully. Last night her dreams had begun to be realized and this morning the whole world was wonderful, or would be if she weren't teetering on the brink of disaster. "I'm mad, that's what I am, raving mad," she muttered as the freezing water ran over her. "I had six years of that man. You'd think I'd have learned my lesson. You'd think I'd know better than to even read a script he was connected with."

She emerged from the shower vigorously toweling her hair. As she came up for air her eyes fell on a large color photograph directly in front of her. It showed a young man with dark hair and laughing blue eyes.

He had a curious face. Most people unthinkingly called him handsome, and he could give the impression of dramatic good looks. But his mobile features were irregular and, as Toni frequently reminded herself, they fell short of the highest standards. A perceptive theater critic had once described Flynn Rawley's face as a combination of the two masks of the drama, tragedy and comedy. He could switch from one to the other with devastating suddenness.

This photograph showed the mask of comedy, capturing Flynn's wicked charm with uncanny accuracy.

He looked like a man who'd eaten the Apple of Life and then planted the seeds in hope. It was precisely that look that had made Toni, against her better judgment, select this picture to adorn her bedroom. Illogically, it incensed her now. "You needn't sit there laughing at me," she said to him severely. "I don't know why I've kept you there."

She looked down at herself. Even in a photograph the devil that lurked in Flynn's eyes could make her intensely conscious of her own nakedness. She threw the towel at the picture so that it landed covering his face, and hiding her decently from view. It was typical of Flynn's attitude that the towel immediately fell off.

Toni was five-foot-two and slightly built. Her usual rehearsal garb of jeans and old shirt made her look boyish, and her short red hair added to the urchinlike appearance. But beneath the clothes her body had a feminine roundness that only Flynn had discovered, and those who assumed from a distance that she was a boy discovered their mistake when they were given the full force of her blue eyes, which were enormous in her tiny, heart-shaped face.

Her eyes were her chief claim to beauty. They glowed with ardor when she was talking about one of her passions, and Toni was passionate about everything. She was passionate about the theater, everyone she met in it, and her own work. She was passionately for things or passionately against them. She didn't know how to be neutral, but attacked life with a fierce enthusiasm that, as Flynn had often complained, was exhausting to everyone else.

Once she'd been passionate about Flynn Rawley. She'd met him when she was seventeen, and from the first moment she'd been blinded by his glory. In those days she'd lived in Farrowdale, a small village in the north of England. She was a secretary for an insurance firm and lived with an aunt who was gently nudging her toward marriage with the boy next door.

Photographs of Toni at that time showed a girl with a pale, eager face gazing anxiously out onto the world. She looked as if she were searching for a miracle that would take her away from the hated job and the narrow limits of her existence. The miracle had arrived in the shape of Flynn Rawley, an actor who'd been briefly engaged by the repertory company of a large town twenty miles away. To her dazzled eyes he'd seemed like a knight in shining armor. He'd ridden to her rescue—not on a white charger, but on a battered old motorbike with which he'd nearly knocked her down.

He was twenty-two, built like a bean pole and had a runaway tongue that he'd inherited from his Irish ancestors. After the first evening Toni understood the expression "kissed the Blarney stone," for no man had ever been more full of blarney than Flynn.

Toni's aunt, a prosaic lady, had called him "that madman who can't stop talking." But to Toni's enchanted ears Flynn's talk had been like outpourings from heaven. After their first encounter she'd spent every penny she earned going to watch his performances. They'd meet afterward, and the night would end with her returning to Farrowdale riding behind him on his scooter in the early hours of the morning.

By the end of the first week she was madly in love—not just with Flynn, but with his whole theatrical world. The thought of going back to her dreary little office was intolerable. When he returned to London at the end of his engagement she begged to go with him.

At first he'd refused. Toni had charmed him but he wasn't ready for that kind of responsibility. Only when she promised not to be a nuisance had he agreed.

For a short while she'd had a blissful, unflawed happiness such as was given to few people, and she knew would never come to her again. The first time Flynn made love to her the stars seemed to stop in their tracks. Nothing mattered except the unbearably sweet poignancy to be found in his arms. At twenty-two he was an enthusiastic lover rather than a subtle one, but always generous.

She'd given Flynn her uncritical adoration, and he'd accepted it with good-humored grace. She was too young and happy to see any fault in this arrangement. But gradually she'd become aware of something wrong. Although Flynn seemed easy to live with, he was disturbingly elusive. He could laugh at poverty, insecurity and disappointment, but his lightheartedness had a defensive quality that kept her at a distance. Toni would have loved to console him for his rare failures, but he seemed able to easily cope alone.

Even more disconcerting was his habit of vanishing behind other personalities. He could adopt any accent at will and switch from naïveté to cynicism, from casual charm to fiery rage, from passion to seeming indifference. Then he could drop all these masks in an instant, revealing that the man behind them was someone else.

But who was he? Often Toni wasn't sure, and as time went on she began to wonder if Flynn himself knew the answer.

When they'd been together six months he'd put on a huge moustache, gone down on one knee and proposed to her in an excruciating accent. She'd accepted quickly, before he could pass it off as a joke and to this day she didn't know if he'd really meant it or not.

Flynn was a born flirt and marriage hadn't changed him. Although Toni knew in her heart that he was faithful, she suffered torments of jealousy. But she kept them to herself, because even as his wife she instinctively tried not to be a nuisance.

He'd taught her the rudiments of stage technique and she'd started to get acting jobs of her own. Her small successes boosted her confidence, and gradually her career began to matter for its own sake. Flynn passed from encouragement to annoyance. He was doing well by then, and couldn't see why she would leave him to take minor engagements at the other end of the country.

Once, he'd persuaded her to refuse a good part in the provinces and instead take a small role in his own London play. She'd been thrilled at working with him—until she discovered that he'd engineered it to keep her at home. When she exploded with wrath Flynn had laughed as he always did. But the laughter died on his lips in the face of the tirade she'd hurled at him.

They'd been together for four years, and suddenly the separate strands of her unhappiness had twisted into a knot within her: four years of living in his shadow, of knowing that her joy depended on him while his didn't depend on her; four years of trying not to feel ordinary next to the Beautiful People, who were his natural friends, and of suppressing her jealousy so as not to bore him.

Once the dam had burst the flood had been unstoppable. "I'm tired of clinging to the great Flynn Rawley's coattails," she cried. "I'm tired of suffocating in your clouds of glory. I want some glory of my own."

It had been the first of many terrible arguments. At first they all ended in bed and their rage was consumed by the blazing joy of the flesh that still united them. But the fights grew worse. He was bewildered by her anger, unable to understand that she wanted to prove herself his equal in the theater. One day, bored by yet another quarrel, he resorted to clowning. Producing his worst stage Irish, he cringed in mock terror and whined, "Ah now, ye wouldn't be gettin' mad at me, would ye, me darlin'?"

"For God's sake, stop it!" she cried. "Stop hiding behind other people. Why can't you have the honesty to be yourself sometimes?"

She thought for a moment that she'd broken through his guard when he paled at her words. But then he gave a short laugh and wryly said, "Perhaps I'm not an honest man. After all, telling lies for a living isn't a very honest profession. We're not called rogues and vagabonds for nothing." His eyes narrowed, "You shouldn't have married an actor, Toni. You should have married a civil servant who could leave his work at the office."

He walked out immediately, giving her no time to reply. He didn't return until the early hours, and she could tell by his movements that he'd been drinking.

They'd made up the next day, but they could see the fear in each other's eyes, and that night when he reached for her she froze. That, too, was the first of many occasions. Soon afterward she left him, and it had felt like escape.

She gave up acting to become a director and knew at once that she'd found her true vocation. But even without her job, she'd never have regretted her impulsive decision of ten years ago. Her love might have failed in the end, but it had given her laughter, fevered nights and moments of heart-stopping joy. She had memories that filled her with intense gratitude toward Flynn and made her forgive him everything. She'd never forget or regret him. She'd be his stay in times of trouble; if he was in need he could have her last penny, if he was ill she'd chain herself to his sickbed.

But hell would freeze over before she'd work with him.

She dressed hurriedly in jeans and sweater and threw on a jacket. She had just time to dash down to the newsstand for the early-evening paper before the messenger arrived with the script. She hurried up the steps of her basement apartment, taking deep, joyous lungfuls of the bright autumn air. A quick sprint to the shop, and she was back in ten minutes. She ran harder the last few hundred yards because she could see a motorbike by the curb.

Her heart nearly stopped when she saw the messenger himself, seated on the bottom step, leaning against her front door. He looked old and frail, and seemed to be laboring under some distress. "Are you all right?" Toni asked worriedly as she reached him.

A bout of coughing shook the old man. "I will be," he managed to whisper at last. "If I could just come inside for a moment."

She opened the door quickly and gave him her arm. As they went inside he bent double with another storm of coughing, and almost collapsed into a kitchen chair. Through the frantic wheezing Toni managed to make out, "one of me turns." She thumped him on the back. "Thank you, sonny," the old man grunted at last.

"Miss," she said shortly.

"Eh?"

"It's miss. I'm female. Miss Antonia Locksley."

He studied the name on the package in his hand. "Is this you? Toni Locksley?"

"That's me." She relieved him of it. "You'd better have some tea." She put the kettle on the stove and set the table with two cups.

"Yes, you are," the old man suddenly said.

"I beg your pardon?"

"Female. I can see it now you've taken your jacket off. Don't know what the world's coming to. In my day women looked like women and you knew where you were. They had female names too. Toni! What sort of name is that for a lass?"

"What's *your* name?" she asked, to divert him.

"Jim."

"Well, Jim, you shouldn't be doing this kind of job at all at your age. You should be putting your feet up."

"So I should. But I've had a string of bad luck, sir... miss... madam..."

"Toni," she said, chuckling.

"I've had bad luck, Toni. Is that my tea? Four spoonfuls please." He watched as Toni ladled sugar into his cup. "Ta. You're a real lady, even if you do look like a lad. He was wrong about you."

"Who?"

"The one who's going to be in this." Jim stabbed the script with a grimy finger. "Calls himself an actor. Couldn't act his way out of a paper bag if you ask me."

"You mean Flynn Rawley?"

"That's the fellow. You knew who it was as soon as I said he couldn't act, didn't you?"

"Well...I don't know about that. He's highly thought of."

"Not by me," Jim said firmly. "I saw him on the telly the other night. Nothing but a pretty face."

"He's not even a pretty face," Toni said. "He cons people into thinking he's handsome, but actually his nose is too big and his mouth's too wide. But never mind that. What's he been saying about me?"

"He talks about you something scandalous. But don't you worry. I'll go back and tell him you ain't really as hard as nails—"

"What?"

"He don't want you on this play," Jim said with relish. "Said you was a real Miss Bossyboots, and didn't know nothin' about the theater. Here, are you all right? You look as sick as a parrot."

"I'm fine, thank you," Toni said, breathing hard. "Just go on."

"Well, that's it. Mr. Dunway said he wanted you, but this Flynn feller's hoping you say no. *Hey!*" Jim jumped violently as he turned to look at something he'd noticed out of the corner of his eye. "Ain't that his picture?"

Toni followed his gaze, and realized that he could see across the hall and into her bedroom. "Here, what are you doing with his picture if you two are slanging each other off?" His voice rose a note in puritan outrage. "Are you his fancy piece? 'Cos I don't hold with goings-on."

"No, I'm not his 'fancy piece,'" Toni said, looking at Jim curiously. "I'm his ex-wife."

"Aha! But you kept his picture. You're still spoony on him, ain't you?"

"Certainly *not*. On the contrary, I think leaving him was the best day's work I ever did. That man is a thoroughly unscrupulous fraud, and I've only just realized how low he can sink."

As she spoke she moved determinedly toward Jim. He viewed her with alarm and edged away frantically. "Here..." he yelped. "What you doin'? Keep your hands off me, you brazen hussy—*ow!*"

This cry of agony was torn from him as Toni seized his moustache and wrenched it off in one piece. She stood there holding her trophy triumphantly while her victim rubbed his upper lip.

"You ought to be shot, Flynn Rawley," she said.

Two

Before her indignant eyes "Jim" rose from his chair and straightened up. As if by magic the elderly body vanished to be replaced by a tall young man who stood looking down at her from laughing blue eyes. He still wore the peaked cap with wisps of gray hair escaping from under it, and he seemed to have rubbed dust into his skin to disguise his fresh complexion, but there was no doubt this was Flynn Rawley—sheepish, but typically unrepentant. "You nearly tore my lip off," he grumbled.

"It's a pity you weren't wearing a beard as well, then I could have done the job properly," she said, with cheerful callousness.

"You're a hard-hearted woman."

He vanished into the bathroom and reappeared a moment later. The wig was gone, revealing his own black hair combed into some semblance of order, and his face was clean of spirit gum and dust. The change in him was astonishing, but Toni, a fair-minded woman, had to admit that the transformation had little to do with false hair. Flynn had become an old man by his gait and his voice. How protective she'd felt toward that frail figure! The thought that he'd been secretly laughing incensed her all over again. "What sort of game do you think you're playing?" she demanded.

"I'm not playing. I came to deliver your script."

"Since when was that the job of the leading man?"

"Well, I must admit I had an ulterior motive."

"I can't recall the last time you did anything without an ulterior motive."

"I thought if I could make you mad enough you'd take the job, just to show me."

"Did you have to indulge in that dreadful ham performance?"

"Ah now, be fair! I fooled you for a while."

She laughed reluctantly. "All right. You took me in until you turned your head suddenly and I saw your earlobes. You told me yourself, once, that no man can change the shape of his ears. Mind you, I began to suspect when you had all that sugar. I remembered your enormous sweet tooth, and how cross I used to be that you could eat whatever you liked without putting on a pound."

At thirty-two, Flynn was almost as lean as he'd been ten years ago. His face, too, had retained its youthful cast, although the first lines were beginning to come. But even these were mainly laugh lines. Laughter was as much a part of Flynn's life as breathing.

He'd been away making a film and Toni hadn't seen him for eight months. Now he was a sight for sore eyes, lighting up her little basement kitchen just by standing there. It was always hard for Toni to meet him again after an absence, for then the impact of his disturbing presence would strike her afresh with almost as much force as on the first day she saw him. He'd smile at her with a particular gleam in his eye and suddenly she was an awkward seventeen-year-old again, breathless at the eruption of this wonderful being into her life.

She could cope with this reaction now by reminding herself that it would soon pass and she'd be her normal sane self again. But it irked her that after all this time Flynn's spell could still catch her off guard. She began to grumble to cover the fact that her heart was beating a little faster. "I suppose I should have expected some daft trick like this."

"Yes, you should, shouldn't you?" he said, apparently serious. "Really, Toni, where were your wits to let me take you by surprise so easily?"

She was torn between exasperation and amusement. "Well, I wasn't expecting you. I thought you were still abroad making that film."

"But Shep told you this morning that he'd talked to me first."

"I thought he meant he'd spoken to you on the phone. You ought to be miles away."

"No, I got home yesterday evening. I meant to come to your opening, but I dropped in on Mel about ten minutes before he had his heart attack, so I never got to the play. Sorry I missed your big moment. Never mind. We'll make up for it with this play."

"Flynn..."

"Look, how about another cup of tea," he said quickly.

"All right. I need it after a shock like this." She went to the stove. "It wasn't a bad piece of acting," she admitted, large-mindedly, "but your scriptwriter was a terrible ham."

He grinned. "I got carried away. I wouldn't have missed the sight of your face for anything in the world. Besides, I thought it might serve as my audition."

"What do you mean?"

"Shep told me how you nearly fainted with horror at the idea of working with me, so I thought since you evidently don't rate me as an actor I'd show you what I can do."

"Don't be absurd. It wasn't that. You're a fine actor. I just don't think we can work together."

"Why?"

"Flynn, you're just pretending to be obtuse."

"It's not a pretense, I swear it," he said at once.

Her lips twitched. "Oh, you're impossible. You know perfectly well what I mean."

Flynn didn't answer. He sat watching Toni as she moved about the kitchen, noticing the little signs that showed the strain she'd been under. Long rehearsals had made her lose weight and there were smudges under her eyes. "You don't look so good," he said at last.

"I'm worn out. You know how it is with the last weeks of rehearsal."

"And you haven't been eating properly. I can tell. You always used to force food down me, but who looks after you?"

"I don't need anyone to look after me," Toni said firmly.

A look of sadness and irony shadowed Flynn's face. It ended in a wry smile, either at himself or her, and even that was quickly banished before she could turn and see it. He began to look around the little apartment. "You weren't living here when I last saw you."

"I got it four months ago, when I was offered *Dead And Alive*."

"The fruits of success, huh?" Flynn said, glancing at a torn spot on the wallpaper.

"To me, yes. Of course I realize that to you it's but a mere shack—"

"Don't get defensive," he broke in hastily.

"Well, don't make faces at my lovely apartment. I know it needs a little redecorating, but I'm very proud of it."

"All right, all right," he said, putting up his hands placatingly. "I just think it's ridiculous for you to live in a place like this when you could have something much nicer."

"You mean, if I took money from you?"

"Yes. You've every right to it." No matter how Flynn had insisted, she hadn't taken a penny from him, even in their first days apart, and this had always upset him.

"It wouldn't be the same to me. I earned this place myself, that's why it means so much. You should understand that. Don't you remember how proud you were when you bought our first house?"

His eyes lit up. "You're right, it was a dreadful little hovel, wasn't it? But we earned it ourselves."

"*You* earned it. I contributed about fourpence."

He shrugged. "You...me, it was the same thing. On the day we moved in we'd hardly a penny left. You managed to scrape up just enough money to buy some eggs, and I picked you up to carry you over the threshold..."

"And I was so startled that I dropped the eggs," she remembered. "We starved that night."

"Only for food," he said with an evocative smile. "I don't think we even noticed."

She joined in his laughter and then abruptly turned away to the stove so that he wouldn't see her face as the laughter died. She wished he hadn't brought back memories of those happy days. His words—"You... me, it was the same thing"—had hurt her unaccountably. Had they really been that close?

"Tell me what else you've been doing," he said as she set the teapot on the table.

"Working. There hasn't been time for much else."

"What about your encounter with Randy Sandy?"

She gave a faint choke. "Randy Sandy" was Alexander Cade, the actor who'd tried to take her to bed as the price of letting her direct him. "I see Shep's told you."

"Just the outlines." Flynn seemed absorbed in spooning sugar into his tea. "Want me to rearrange his face for you?"

"No thanks, I did that," she said calmly. "Not his face exactly, but the wrist of his contract-signing hand."

He looked chagrined. "Don't you think you could flatter my vanity by pretending to need my help just a little, for old times' sake?"

"That would be a bit silly after my judo lessons, wouldn't it?"

He looked at her. "Things must be pretty bad if you need judo. How long have you been studying?"

"Six months. It helps to know I can take care of myself."

"Can you? How good are you?"

"I could toss you over my shoulder."

He raised an eyebrow incredulously. It irked her more than it should have, as it recalled the times when he'd never quite taken her achievements seriously. "I could," she repeated firmly. "I know you're nearly a foot taller than me but that doesn't matter in judo. I've learned how to use my opponent's weight against him."

"Just the same..." Flynn laughed, shrugging her off dismissively.

Toni leapt to her feet. "All right," she said crossly. "Get up and attack me."

"Forget it, pet."

"Get up! And don't call me pet."

With a wry face Flynn got to his feet. His turn was so swift that she never saw it. In a second they were both on the floor, but she was flat on her back, her legs trapped between Flynn's, and both her hands imprisoned in his. "I'm sorry, pet," he laughed. "It was rotten of me not to mention that I've studied judo, too."

"You—that was cheating!"

"How so? Your next attacker might know judo and then where would you be?"

She struggled to free herself but it was useless. Flynn's thighs enclosed hers in an unbreakable hold, and her movements against him only reminded her of the wiry strength of his lean body. The abrupt close physical contact after so long was unnerving. At last she gave up fighting and stared up at him furiously. "Will you let me up, please?" she said through gritted teeth.

He grinned, looking down appreciatively at her flushed cheeks and disheveled hair. "Make me!"

"*Flynn!* I said, let me up!"

Her exertions had left her breathless and her breasts were rising and falling quickly against her thin sweater. The smile faded from Flynn's face.

"Yes, of course," he said abruptly, and released her. He got up without looking at her. He was shaken by how frail and defenseless she'd felt in his hands. It was easy for her to laugh about her battles with the predators of the theatrical jungle, but he didn't feel like laughing.

"You were provoking me on purpose, weren't you?" she demanded as she rose and brushed herself off.

"Yes. I still feel protective toward you and wanted to judge your skill for myself. You've got a long way to go yet. I'll teach you some new moves while we're working on the show."

"I'm not doing the show. I've already told you."

Flynn took both her hands in his and pulled her down until she was sitting close to him. "Listen, Toni, it's time to be serious. You're at a crossroads in your career. You've had a success that will open doors for you, but you haven't arrived yet. If you turn this down, what will you do?"

"I'll take something else. I'll have other offers."

"Of course you will, but they won't be as big as this one. You won't get to the very top by throwing away your chances."

She was silent. She knew every word he said was true, but she couldn't work with Flynn; he affected her too strongly. Even though she was no longer in love with him, he had a magnetism that she couldn't ignore. She'd sworn to put him out of her life, and the past few minutes had reinforced that decision. For a moment, as she lay on the floor, she'd been giddy with the sense of the past rushing back. He had smiled down at her in a way she remembered, but then she'd seen the laughter drain from his face, leaving behind a blankness that chilled her heart.

"Toni," Flynn said, giving her hands a little shake. "Toni, you're miles away." She tried to free her hands but he held fast. "You ought to listen to me, I'm your Svengali."

"You are?"

"I was the one who first made you think of directing, wasn't I? I said that was where your real talent lay."

She laughed shakily. "Well, that was the gist of it. Your actual words were that I had the soul of a dictator and ought to get to the other side of the footlights before somebody threw me there."

He cleared his throat awkwardly. "Yes... well, now I'm going to make you an offer you can't refuse. If you'll agree to do this show, I'll back out."

"Back out? What are you talking about?"

"You're hesitating on my account, so if I'm not in the show you'll have a clear field."

"Flynn, don't be absurd. They need you far more than they need me."

"No, they don't. There's been someone else nibbling at it." He mentioned a leading man whose name was almost as starry as his own. "He'll leap at the chance, and you'll find him very easy to work with."

Her mind was whirling. This was the last thing she'd expected. To give herself time to think she seized on another detail. "Haven't you signed a contract?"

He grinned wickedly. "I've got the best agent in the business. That contract is full of holes."

"But Shep's counting on you. You couldn't let him down."

"He's counting on you, too, but you're ready to do just that. If I'm causing the problem, I'll get out."

She stared at him. "You really mean it, don't you?"

"I'm not joking now. This is your big chance."

"Flynn, I couldn't possibly let you leave just to make way for me."

"You couldn't actually stop me."

"Oh yes, I could. I could say I won't do it without you."

She caught herself up as she realized what she was saying. Flynn's lips were pressed together as though he were trying to stop himself laughing, and his eyes were full of mischief. "I walked straight into that one, didn't I?" She sighed.

His mercurial brain had always been able to think rings around her more methodical one. She was analytical, enjoying the process of dissecting a play, or a role, to see what made it work. Flynn relied on his brilliant instincts.

"*If* I agree to do this play, and it's a big if," she said slowly, "you'd have to be part of it. You're ideal for the role."

"You don't know that. You haven't read the script yet."

"No, but I've read *Much Ado*. You were born to play Benedick."

"If you think that," he said, serious again, "then perhaps we really can work together. Why don't you have a look at the script?"

As soon as she opened *The Merry War* she began to feel the excitement. This was potentially a great show. From Shakespeare's play the author had cleverly filleted the charming story of Beatrice and Benedick, two lovers who concealed their feelings behind a mask of defensive banter, until circumstances forced them into the open.

A lot would depend on the music, but the lyrics were subtle and witty. Images began to dance through her head. She knew just what would make this work, how it ought to look, if only...

"I can tell you want to do it," Flynn said, reading her face with the intuitive understanding that could make him a hair-raising companion. "It's written all over you."

"Yes, I do," Toni said honestly. "But there's another problem. The fact is, I'm probably getting married again soon."

Flynn was pouring tea into her cup. "So?" he said without looking at her.

"Well, for heaven's sake! This is hardly the time for me to go to work with my ex-husband."

Flynn gave her a wry look. "Haven't you forgotten something? You told 'Jim' that you were my ex-wife, but weren't you being a bit premature?"

"*Almost* ex-wife," she amended hastily.

He grinned. "It does make a difference, you know. Even in these permissive times it's usual to get a divorce before taking another husband. I forget now why we neglected that formality..."

"We were going to divorce by consent after being apart for two years," Toni said. "But when the two years were up I could never pin you down. You were always off on the other side of the world, and somehow time slipped by. Most people think we *are* divorced."

"What about your potential second husband? Does he know you're still married to me?"

"Of course he does. I wouldn't deceive Alec."

"Ah, so his name's Alec?"

"Alexander Wrighton. He's a stockbroker."

"Sounds like a good, solid character," Flynn said, assuming a mocking expression.

"He is," Toni said firmly.

"If he's the least bit fond of you he won't want to stand in the way of your career. Or does he want you to give it up?"

"Flynn, it isn't like that. I only said I *might* be getting married. He hasn't asked me properly. We've only just sort of... edged around it."

"But you think he'd object to your working with me? Why on earth should he?"

"Why?" She stared at him.

"I'm serious. The past is over."

She hesitated. Was the past really dead when she could shy away so nervously from the thought of working with him?

"Of course it is," she forced herself to say firmly. "You shouldn't read anything into that picture I keep. It's just for old times' sake."

"That's what I thought," he said demurely, but his eyes danced.

"Oh no, you didn't," she said with remembered indignation. "You tried to get me to say I was still spoony on you."

"Well, you didn't say it," murmured Flynn wryly.

"What was that?"

"Nothing. Are you in love with this...stockbroker?" He said the word as if it left a bad taste in his mouth.

"I don't think that's any of your business," Toni told him firmly.

Flynn seemed to appeal to heaven. "My wife tells me to my face that it's none of my business if she's in love with another man. I don't know what the modern woman is coming to."

"Oh, be serious. You know what I mean. We're more like brother and sister."

His glance was cynical, but he only said, "And like a good brother I'm keeping a protective eye on you." Without warning, Flynn aged twenty years, looking down his nose and speaking in a pompous neigh. "I know what appalling taste in men you have, m'dear. Couldn't stand that actor chappie of yours. Fellers wearin' makeup and fancy dress: dashed bad form y'know. In my day he'd have been horsewhipped. Eh, what?"

Toni's lips twitched. "I'm glad you see my ex-husband so clearly."

Flynn stopped playing. "So now, answer me. Are you in love with him?"

"You don't think I could be, do you?" she asked crossly. "You think once a woman's been in love with you she's yours for life."

Flynn gave her a strange look. "Is that a challenge?"

"No, it isn't," she said, backing down hastily.

"It sounded very like one to me, and you know I could never resist a dare. Is it the same with him as it was with us?"

She gave a jerky little laugh. "I'm not sure what you mean. I never really knew how it was with us."

Before she guessed what he meant to do Flynn reached out, took her by the shoulders and drew her close to him. "It was like this," he said as he brought his mouth down to hers.

She made an instinctive sound of protest and raised her hands to push him away. But he placed his arms around her, and held her in a grip of steel while he pressed his lips insistently against hers. Rage possessed her. How *dared* Flynn do such a thing! Suddenly her senses swam at the feel of his firm flesh. How she'd loved to caress it at one time, and how he'd loved her, too.

It was infamous of him to bring those memories back to her. Her fury flowed through her like a stream, flooding her body with adrenaline, causing it to quicken with an excitement that was much like the excitement of love.

His mouth was teasing, coaxing her to soften and surrender to him, but she hardened herself against the dangerous beguilement. Flynn had one arm beneath her neck and the other pressed into the small of her back, crushing her against his hard frame. He was imprisoning her in the most unscrupulous way, knowing that she couldn't do a thing about it.

Or could she? The memory of Flynn's secret weakness suddenly came back to her. Moving slowly, not to alarm him, she positioned her hands on his ribs and attacked.

He gave a bellow of outrage and leapt back from her, dodging madly to avoid her tickling. *"Get off!"* he yelled. "Keep away from me, d'you hear?"

She lunged for him again, fingers working madly. "Serves you right," she told him breathlessly. "I'll teach you to play rotten tricks—"

"What do you call this?"

"You asked for it!"

"All right, all right!" Flynn had retreated till he was against a wall and succeeded in taking hold of her wrists. "I give up. Pax?"

"Pax. And don't you ever dare try a thing like that again."

He looked sheepish. "I'm sorry, Toni. I know it was wrong but I couldn't resist it. I guess you're right about me—I'm just a dog in the manger. I don't like the thought that what was mine once isn't mine any longer."

"Considering how little you wanted it while you had it, I don't see why you bother," she said.

He gave her a strange look that she pretended not to notice. She refused to question his silence, fearing that he'd only agree that he indeed had never loved her. *I'm a fool,* she thought. *What did I think he was going to say?*

She turned away from him. She was still in the grip of the heady excitement of anger, and she could feel the flush in her cheeks. She knew Flynn would mistake the cause of her agitation.

"You still haven't told me if you're in love with Alec," Flynn said. "Or shall I let you off that awkward question?"

"It's not awkward at all," she said defiantly. "I *am* in love with him and if—*when* he asks me, I'm going to marry him."

The telephone rang, and she snatched up the receiver. "Hello!" she said, more shortly than she'd intended.

"Toni? Is something wrong?" Her caller sounded alarmed at her tone of voice.

"Nothing wrong at all, Alec, dear. I'm glad you called."

"I left it late to give you time to wake up. Congratulations on your reviews, darling. It'll be champagne tonight. You haven't forgotten that we're having dinner after the performance? Last night I had to share you with too many other people."

"Don't worry. Tonight you'll have me all to yourself."

"Good. I'll pick you up at the theater."

She replaced the receiver and turned to find Flynn scowling. "That, I take it, was the stockbroker."

"Yes, that was Alec."

"Alec, who's going to have you all to himself tonight," Flynn said significantly.

Toni chuckled at the sight of his face. "Go away, dog in the manger."

"You ought to be reading this—" Flynn pointed to the script "—not . . . whatever it is you're planning."

She refused to help him out. "I'll have plenty of time to read it before I leave for the theater. I'll start as soon as you've gone, which will be in about five seconds," she said firmly.

He collected his jacket, rammed the cap back on his head at a jaunty angle, and went to the door. "I'll tell Shep you promise him a decision by tomorrow," he said, and vanished before she could protest that this was far too soon.

She stared indignantly at the closed door, seeming to see Flynn's vibrant presence still imprinted on the air where he'd stood. The kitchen was very quiet now he'd gone. She gave herself a little shake. She had no time for daydreaming.

She took up *The Merry War* and tried to read it through calmly, but after a few minutes she realized she wasn't taking anything in. Drat Flynn, she thought, for taking her by surprise and throwing her into disorder. She'd have to try again later that night.

On her way to the theater she dropped into her agent's office and collected three other scripts that had arrived for her. She found boards up in front of the theater bearing quotes from the rave reviews and gazed at them, possessed by blissful pride.

The second night went as well as the first, and as Toni stood in the wings her excitement mounted. She was well on her way to the top. All she needed now was a big hit, and she'd have arrived.

Alec appeared backstage just as the final curtain came down. He stared when he saw the bundle of scripts she was bringing with her. "This is supposed to be a night out," he protested.

"It will be. I'll read those when I get home."

"Don't you ever stop work?"

"Nope. No more than you do," she said with a laugh. "I'd bet money you spent this evening working at the office till it was time to come and meet me."

"Well, I deal in an international market. Stockbrokers expect to work all hours."

"So do theater people," Toni said. Uninvited, the memory of Flynn's words came to mind and she added, a touch belligerently, "Is there any reason why I shouldn't?"

"None at all," Alec said. "You needn't be so touchy, darling."

When they were in the car Toni turned her head to look at Alec, admiring his dignified good looks. He was an imposing man in his forties with quiet manners. She found his calm solidity a delightful change after Flynn's restlessness, and in his company she always felt safe.

They reached the restaurant and were led to the quiet corner table Alec had reserved. "Now tell me what's been upsetting you," he asked.

"Flynn Rawley," she said with a sigh. "All the troubles of my life can be summed up in those two words."

"He's not being difficult about the divorce, is he? You told me it was just a formality."

"It will be. It's not that. He was with me when you rang this afternoon. That was why I snapped when I picked up the phone."

"What did he want?"

"He wants me to direct his next play, of all things. I've tried to make him see that it's impossible, but there's no talking to Flynn when he gets an idea in his head."

"Why is it impossible?"

Toni stared. "Because he's my estranged husband and I'd be working with him closely, for weeks."

"But what does that matter? You're not in love with him anymore, are you?"

"Of course I'm not," she said sharply. "That was all over long ago."

"Then there's no problem."

Toni's head was spinning. "You mean you don't mind?"

Alec gave a quiet chuckle. "Darling, did you think I'd try to talk you out of it because I was afraid of Flynn Rawley?"

"Plenty of men *are* afraid of him," she said, unreasonably nettled by Alec's dismissive tone. "He's considered quite a ladies' man."

"But not to you, surely? I mean, why would he bother?"

Toni ground her teeth, not at all pleased by the turn the conversation was taking.

"Darling," Alec said gently, "don't expect me to be jealous. I've never met him but I know his type and I don't think you could be fooled twice. A man with no sense of purpose—"

"That's not fair. Flynn was always in deadly earnest about his ambition."

"Yes, but what ambition? Dressing up and prancing around onstage? What sort of purpose is that for a man?"

Toni gave a little choke. It was sheer bad luck that Alec's words recalled Flynn's impersonation of a blimpish colonel earlier that day, but the echo was so clear that she had to fight to keep a straight face.

"Have I said something funny?"

"It's not 'prancing around,'" she said hurriedly before Alec could pursue the subject. "A really great actor is a kind of mirror that shows people truths about their own hearts. The ancient Greeks believed drama was valuable because it 'purged the soul with pity and terror,' and if a man can do that, you can't say he hasn't got a serious purpose."

"And is that what Flynn Rawley does?"

"He can, at his best."

"I thought he was mostly a comedy actor."

"Well comedy can make you feel pity and terror as well. It's actually a lot more difficult than tragedy and—"

Alec held up his hands placatingly. "Okay, you can come off that soapbox of yours. I give in."

Toni stared at him as something dawned on her, and she wondered why it had taken so long. "You think the theater's a waste of time, don't you, Alec?"

"Of course not," he said quickly. "I like a good variety show, or something like that. Mind you, I haven't got much time for all this soul searching."

"You mean like the soul searching I did over *Dead and Alive*?" she asked curiously. "Was I boring you?"

"You couldn't bore me," he insisted loyally. "But let's face it, one murder mystery is pretty much like another."

"But it wasn't a murder mystery," Toni said, indignant at being misunderstood. "The killer and the victim were reflections of each other, and the whole play turned on their personalities—"

"You're off again," Alec stopped her with a grin. "Look darling, I'm happy for anything that makes *you* happy. Let's leave it there."

"Yes, perhaps we'd better," she said uneasily. She wondered what ill luck had made the usually charming Alec seem at his worst tonight.

"Why don't we discuss this divorce of yours, all right?" Alec gave a self-conscious smile that made him likable again. "I have a personal interest in it."

"Well, now Flynn's back in London it'll be easier to arrange."

"It can't happen too soon for me. I'm glad you're doing this play with him. It'll complete the process of getting him out of your system."

"But I don't need to 'complete the process,'" she said with a little laugh. "Flynn's been out of my system a long time. I want someone quite different now, someone solid and reliable..." She floundered for the right words.

"Safe and dull?" Alec offered with a twinkle in his eye.

"You're not in the least dull," she said, a little too firmly, "and I could do with some safety."

When they said good-night she kissed Alec warmly, reminding herself that he was a kind man and it wasn't fair to expect a stockbroker to see her job as she did. "Methinks the lady doth protest too much," she imagined Flynn quoting wickedly.

"I really must get home and start working," she said.

The quiet of her apartment was a welcome relief. She settled down, surrounded by scripts. Two of them she discarded after the first act, and one after the first ten minutes. At last she took up *The Merry War* and read it right through. When she'd finished she knew that this was potentially the hit of the season and the making of Toni Locksley. She sat staring at it, torn by indecision. She was shaken by the terrible sense of how much she wanted this success—to prove herself, to have her own moment of glory. This was what she'd dreamed of since the days when she'd stood in the wings and watched Flynn dominate an audience, giving himself to them utterly and winning their adoration in return. This show could give her everything she wanted—but at a cost.

The phone rang, and she lifted the receiver. "Did he give you permission?" Flynn asked.

"I didn't ask his permission," she snapped.

"Of course you didn't. But when you'd finished not asking for it, did he give it?"

Toni clenched her free hand into a fist. "He was delighted for me. He said it would never occur to him to think he had anything to fear from you."

"So you didn't tell him I kissed you?"

"Actually," she said coolly, "I'd forgotten all about that."

There was a silence that made her wish she could see his face. Then he said quietly, "You're a liar, Toni Locksley."

"And you're a conceited . . . ooh, I wish I could get my hands on you!"

"There's nothing stopping you. Turn Alec Wrighton out and I'll come over."

"Alec's not here," she said before she could stop herself. She heard his soft chuckle and knew he'd outthought her again. "Now listen to me, Flynn, I want it clearly understood that just because I was crazy at seventeen doesn't mean I haven't learned any sense since. I am *not* letting you back in my life in any way, shape or form. It's a lovely show and I'm sorry I won't be doing it but there it is. I hope I've made myself clear."

"Perfectly clear. I'll call Shep and tell him you say yes. Bye."

"Flynn!"

But he'd hung up.

Three

Toni visited Mel in the hospital and found him sitting up in bed, looking better than she'd expected of a man of sixty who'd just had a massive heart attack. "Bless you for the flowers, Toni," he said. "Since I can't do *The Merry War* I'm delighted it's going to you."

"I'm already sorry I said yes," she told him. "I'm here to pick your brains, Mel."

"Well, your chief problem is that all the decisions have been made, so you won't get a say in the cast, set designer, choreographer, etcetera."

"That's all right. I've looked over the names and I think they're fine—" Toni hesitated "—all but one."

"Let me guess. Carole Conrad."

"Right," Toni said fervently.

Carole was a young actress of startling beauty. She'd been successful in modern light-comedy roles, but Toni was dismayed to find her cast as Beatrice, which she thought beyond her range. "Of course, I haven't seen a lot of her work," she admitted, trying to be fair, "but she wouldn't have been my first choice for Beatrice."

"She wasn't mine, either, but Flynn persisted."

Toni looked up sharply. "Flynn? But why?"

"Your guess is as good as mine, but he wouldn't do it without her. He insists she's up to it, although no one else thinks she is. They've worked together recently..." He left the implication hanging in the air.

Toni bit her lip. Mel had come within a hair's breadth of saying that Flynn was personally involved with Carole, but it wasn't like him to work with a woman on that account. Beneath his easygoing exterior Flynn was a ruthless professional. "There's a first time for everything," Mel said, reading her expression. "Carole's a very lovely lady."

A week later she met the young actress face to face, at the first rehearsal. Toni arrived early at the old Regent Theatre and waited on the big, draughty stage to greet the cast. She knew they were nervous. They'd felt safe with Mel, a director with a string of West End hits behind him, but now their employment depended on a virtual unknown. Small wonder if they regarded her with only half-friendly curiosity. Toni maintained a smiling and composed front, but inwardly she, too, was shaking. It would have been nice to talk to Flynn and have him laugh her fears away as he'd often done in their happy days.

At that moment she looked up and saw him coming in with Carole Conrad. His arm was around her shoulders, and he was smiling at her reassuringly. Toni heard him say, "Don't be scared. She's not an ogre."

Thanks, Flynn, thought Toni grimly.

"Toni, this is Carole Conrad," Flynn said, coming toward her.

The two women shook hands and Toni shifted uncomfortably as she took in the young actress's glowing beauty. Carole was dark and willowy, with a shy smile and graceful movements. She towered seven inches above Toni and could almost look Flynn in the eye. Toni talked to her for a few minutes, then watched her float elegantly away in Flynn's direction.

"They look fantastic together, don't they?" She turned and saw Theo Carter, the costume designer, a small, bald man in his fifties. He thrust some drawings into her hand and sighed, "Those two are a dream to design for."

"They're rather alike," Toni said critically. "Shouldn't there be some contrast?"

"Who needs contrast when people suit each other like they do? Don't you see what a perfect pair they make?"

"Yes, I do." She hadn't meant to sound so short and became absorbed in studying the designs.

When everyone was present Toni sat them in a semicircle while she stood before them and made a short speech, introducing herself. "Today I'd like to do a verbal run-through," she finished. "Stay sitting where you are and say your lines, but get up for the songs if you want to. Duff will kick off by playing us the overture." She smiled at the composer, Duff Briarley, who was sitting at the upright piano. His lyricist, who was also his wife, Joanna, was leaning over the top.

At the first bars of the overture Toni felt a tingle go up her spine. Even without an orchestra the score was magic. The company thought so, too, because when the music stopped they applauded. This broke some of the ice and she breathed more freely as they began to read their lines. But Toni felt a cold lump at the pit of her stomach at the sound of Carole Conrad's stiff, lifeless voice. Why had Flynn insisted on having her cast as Beatrice?

"Benedick" appeared and became engaged in a witty exchange with "Beatrice." Flynn delivered the lines in a polished manner that showed he'd worked on them, and Toni remembered how meticulously he'd always planned for a first rehearsal. "It impresses the director no end," he'd once said flippantly. She wondered if he was trying to impress her.

She soon became convinced that he was. The touch of peevishness he injected into "It is certain I am loved of all ladies, only you excepted" made the company rock with laughter, in which Toni gladly joined. Flynn raised an ironic eyebrow in her direction.

"Thank you, Flynn," she said in her best directorial manner. "I promise you I'm *very* impressed."

His lips twitched, and she knew that he'd picked up the echo.

Then Carole Conrad spoke again and Toni groaned inwardly. How could she say "I had rather hear my dog bark at a crow than a man swear he loves me," in such a flat voice, and show so little response to Flynn's delightful raillery? But Toni held her tongue. These were early days.

She relaxed a little when Carole began to sing in her clear, well-controlled soprano. Flynn's pleasant light baritone joined her in duet and their voices blended well. But as the read-through continued Toni became gradually aware of another worry: there was something indefinably wrong about the show as it stood. The script was clever, the songs witty and tuneful, yet a vital link had been missed out on, and she couldn't pinpoint it.

That evening she went home and brooded, knowing she was facing her first major test. During rehearsals a musical resembled a half-prepared dish. Ingredients would be added or removed as the players showed their talents. Gradually the dish would firm into shape, become crisp at the edges and acquire a golden look. But it could only happen if the director was a good cook, and suddenly Toni had a sickening sense of her own inadequacy.

I can't do it, she thought with a fluttering of panic. I'm too inexperienced and they all know I am. If we fail, it'll be my fault.

The next day she took Flynn and Carole through one of their early scenes, trying to control her frustration at Carole's awkwardness. During the lunch break Flynn dropped into a seat beside her, handing her a plastic cup full of coffee. "Thanks," she said, gulping it gratefully. "Flynn, we're going to have problems with Carole."

His face darkened slightly. "Give her time," he begged. "That's all she needs."

"I think she's out of her depth."

"I've worked with her before. When she gets going she'll give a performance that will bring out the best in me. That's why I wanted her."

"Hmm!"

"What's that supposed to mean?"

"Not another of your flirtations is it?" she asked, trying to sound casual.

"One of my flirtations?" He frowned as if trying to remember. "Wait while I check the files. . . ."

Toni matched his playful tone with her own. "I can well believe that you can't carry them all in your head, Don Juan, but I do think the current one should stand out a little from the others."

"Ah," he said craftily, "but who says she *is* the current one?"

Toni put her head close to his and spoke in a conspiratorial whisper. "Well, due to the circumstances, don't you think she ought to be?"

"For the good of the show, you mean? I hadn't thought of it, but never let it be said that Flynn Rawley shirked his duty." He solemnly kissed her hand. "For you, Toni, anything."

He departed with an air of noble self-sacrifice, leaving Toni suppressing a grin and wondering what she had to do to outthink Flynn.

Carole seemed to cling to him for reassurance. Once, when Toni praised her for some small improvement, the actress instinctively looked at him, and it was his smile and nod that made her relax. "She's improving, I'll grant you," Toni said during the break a few days later, "but not nearly fast enough."

"Why are you so unjust?" Flynn demanded. "Carole's not the first actor you've know who takes time to warm up. What about Fred Belton in *Dead and Alive*? If you could be patient with him, why not with Carole?"

"That's different," she said quickly.

"Why?"

She hurriedly pushed away the shocking thoughts of her jealousy. "I chose Fred myself," she said, "knowing his problems, but knowing how talented he was. Carole was forced on me by you, though I can't imagine why."

"Can't you? I thought you'd persuaded yourself that I was having an affair with her?" he said lightly.

"I don't need much persuading when I see how bad she is. I resent the fact that you allowed your personal feelings to interfere with this show."

Flynn's eyes kindled in a rare display of temper. "I thought you were joking before, but you mean it, don't you? Toni, are you crazy? When we were together you used to complain that I forgot everything else when I was working? You said I was ruthless, and you were damned right. I'll do anything I have to to get the best out of myself and I let *nothing* stand in the way of that best. Do you really think I'd risk my reputation with an incompetent leading lady just so that I could...?" Words failed him.

Toni got up abruptly and went to the coffee machine feeling very foolish. Everything Flynn said was true. He was a steely professional, with a well-developed instinct for survival.

When she came back Flynn was still there. He looked at her wryly, but the anger was gone. She handed him a coffee as a peace offering, and he made a play of tasting it carefully. "You needn't worry. I haven't got the arsenic with me today," she said.

"That's a relief. You're such a goose, Toni."

The unexpected tenderness in his voice made her heart lurch alarmingly. He looked at her a moment. "At this point a vain man might wonder if you were jealous," he ventured.

"He'd have to be very vain indeed to think that," she assured him.

"Or very human. I don't much like *your* being in love with someone else. It would be only friendly if you'd feel the same way."

"As long as it doesn't affect the show, your love life is of no interest to me," she told him firmly.

"Now, there we differ, because I do care where your stockbroker spends his nights."

He was still smiling and his tone was light, but his eyes held a strange gleam. Toni faced him defiantly and said nothing. "Tell me," he persisted.

"Flynn, stop this. We have to work together, and that's going to be impossible if our personal lives keep getting dragged in."

"But life isn't a matter of separate compartments, Toni. We once meant the whole world to each other, and you can't just file that away labeled No Longer Applicable. We married very young and we did some growing up together. We shaped each other and we'll carry the imprint of each other all our lives."

She was silent. It was all true.

Flynn touched her cheek gently with a finger. "I still care about you, Toni. I always will."

"Hey, are you two getting together again?" They both jumped at the sight of Gary Arlen, who was handling publicity.

Flynn drew back his hand quickly.

Gary was young, bright, and had the dubious gift of setting people's teeth on edge. He was displaying it to the fullest today. "I keep getting calls from the press," he said in his braying voice. "Everyone thought you were divorced, but there's no record of it. So come on, tell."

Toni forced down her irrational bitterness that Gary had arrived at that moment. She could still feel the place on her cheek where Flynn had touched it, and it was hard to think straight. "We're not divorced...yet,'' she said, gathering her wits. ''But we'll be getting around to it any day now.''

''You mean, while you're actually working on the show?'' Gary said eagerly. ''Hey, that might be even better than a reconciliation—or would it?'' His brow wrinkled with the effort of thought.

''Let us know when you've decided which would suit you better,'' Toni said dryly.

''Well, I...hey, you're putting me on, aren't you?'' Gary brayed his delight.

''How did you guess?'' Toni murmured, trying not to meet Flynn's eye.

''If you're getting divorced, how come you were so lovey-dovey just now?'' Gary persisted.

''And how come they didn't strangle you at birth?'' Flynn said pleasantly.

''I'm beginning to wish they had. I've got journalists on the phone all the time wanting to know how you feel about each other, and you're no help.''

''Tell them we're just good friends,'' Flynn said shortly.

When Gary had finally left, Flynn leaned back in his chair stretching out his long, elegant legs and spoke in an elaborately casual voice. ''What about applying for that divorce right now, Toni? After all,'' he went on smoothly pretending not to notice her instant pallor, ''we must put the show first at all times, and if the director and the leading man call each other rude names in court, ticket sales will go through the roof.''

''There'll be no name-calling. It'll be an uncontested divorce, and neither of us will have to appear.''

''But I think I ought to contest it...strictly for the good of the show.'' His eyes dared her.

Toni regarded Flynn cynically. She knew he was only teasing, but even without a fight their divorce now would arouse the kind of interest she didn't want. "We may as well wait," she said coolly.

She thought he was about to reply, but they were interrupted by the production secretary saying Toni was wanted on the phone. She came back five minutes later to find Flynn still there. "What is it?" he asked. "Your eyes are shining.

She took a deep breath. "*Dead and Alive* may be going into the West End."

"That's fantastic!" He enveloped her in a bear hug and she laughingly hugged him back, their earlier bickering forgotten. "Let's have some champagne," he said.

"No—" she stopped him quickly "—don't say anything to the company, Flynn. It's not definite yet."

"All right. For the moment it'll be our secret. Except for your stockbroker, of course. Was he pleased for you?"

"Well. . . I haven't called him yet. He has these long lunches."

Flynn's face showed his wry appreciation of this feeble excuse, but he said nothing.

That afternoon she went through the last scene. Beatrice and Benedick were finally forced to confront the truth of their love. Beatrice tried one more retreat into defensive banter, but Benedick silenced her with the words "Peace, I will stop your mouth" and kissed her.

It had always been hard for Toni to watch Flynn embracing another woman onstage. Now she was pleased to find she could view the whole thing with professional detachment. She made them rehearse the kiss several times and gave detailed notes.

At the end of the day she dismissed the actors and called a meeting of the production staff, Duff and Joanna, Theo, Ellis Granger, who was doing the choreography and George Alladale, her assistant director. She asked their reactions to the day and found their remarks constructive, but an air of unease hung over everyone. They looked expectantly at Toni.

They know something's wrong and I don't know what to do about it, she thought apprehensively. We're a team. Why can't I make myself ask their help?

"Fine, that's all for today," she said firmly.

She was the last to leave the theater and stood on the pavement pulling her coat closer against the nip in the air. She wondered what was the matter with her that she'd succumbed to misgivings at this moment. With luck she might soon have two West End shows running at the same time, yet here she was, alone in the chill twilight, because she had no one to share her joys or her fears with.

On impulse she hailed a passing taxi and went to the little fleapit theater where *Dead And Alive* was playing. Here, at least, she'd find the warmth she craved.

She arrived as the first-act curtain was falling to loud applause. Members of the cast appeared and hugged her. Someone produced a bottle of wine and they all toasted each other. Toni laughed and clinked glasses, gave compliments and received them, but something was missing.

During the final curtain calls she slipped around to the front of house to mingle with the departing crowd, eager to pick up some audience reaction. What she heard pleased her, and she was about to leave when there was a suppressed shriek behind her. She turned and saw Flynn surrounded by eager fans.

She backed quietly away and stood against the wall, watching him. Flynn frankly enjoyed his fame, and he was always delightful to fans who waylaid him, making them feel he was all theirs. It was a feeling that the woman who'd once loved him had never known.

Then he looked up and saw Toni. His smile seemed to reach out and touch her, melting the chill of loneliness that had enveloped her. She smiled back, knowing what had been missing from the evening.

Flynn extricated himself and came toward her. "I was about to come and find you."

"How did you know I'd be here?" she asked through a daze of happiness.

"Where else would you be tonight?" he said in a chiding tone, as if to remind her that they were both of the theater and spoke the same language. "Come on, let's get out of here."

They drove back into the center of town, found a small restaurant and settled in a corner. A large, smiling man bustled over. Flynn greeted him as Gino and ordered the meal. Toni was filled with happy relief that, on this special night, Flynn's friendship hadn't failed her. "Why didn't you tell me you were coming to the play?" she asked.

"I'd hoped you'd invite me. But since you're too mean to offer me a free seat I scraped up the money somehow." Toni chuckled, not fooled by this assumption of poverty. Flynn continued, "I wondered if your stockbroker would be with you tonight."

Toni shrugged. "It's not really his kind of scene." Actually she hadn't called Alec yet.

"No, I knew he wasn't there as soon as I saw that you hadn't changed your clothes."

She was still in her working garb, which was definitely casual. Flynn, too, had on the things he'd worn all day but he contrived to imbue them with his own elegance. Tight-fitting jeans emphasized the lines of his long, muscular thighs, narrow hips and flat stomach. He'd removed his jacket, and the sleeves of his old green shirt were rolled up to the elbows, revealing lean forearms that gave little hint of their steely strength. The appearance of Flynn's whipcord body had always been deceptive, she recalled. How many lovers' games had they played, when she'd struggled to break free, and he'd held her without effort? The fact that she didn't really want to escape only added to their excitement.

The corner was lit only by the little flames of the candles, which cast shadows over Flynn's face. It was easy to see that he wasn't really a handsome man, thought Toni. The tiny flickering flames emphasized the irregularity of his mobile features. But when he smiled at her she realized again that his attraction didn't depend on looks, but on a masculine charm and vitality so magnetic that appearance was irrelevant. She breathed a silent prayer of thanks that she'd recovered from that fever and was now immune.

"If there's any justice in the world, Toni, that production will get into the West End," he said. "You did a wonderful job."

She looked at him warily. "You're just being polite."

"Don't be so touchy. I mean it. You approached it in just the right way, peeling off layers of meaning one by one, until the truth was revealed."

"And what did you think was the truth?" she asked anxiously.

"That the killer and his victim were both dead and alive at the same time—mirror images. I think the killer was really trying to destroy something in himself."

"You didn't think it was just another murder mystery?"

"I suppose that's straight from the stockbroker's mouth," Flynn said shrewdly. "You're going to have a lovely time married to him."

"Never mind that," she said quickly. "I'm thrilled that you understood what I was getting at. It's heartbreaking when you're trying as hard as you know how, and then someone misunderstands."

Unconsciously she'd clenched one hand and given the table a soft thump. Flynn took her hand in both of his. "Actually," he said, "there's danger in trying too hard. You've sometimes been so determined to make the audience see it your way that you've underlined things too much. But with this play you made your points subtly." He released her hand and lifted his glass. "Here's to your success!"

She clinked glasses with him, but her brain was whirring. "Flynn, all my productions have been out in the sticks. But you're talking as though you'd seen them."

"I get around," he said evasively.

"Not to the kind of places *I've* been working. You've been abroad, or acting in London."

"Not every minute."

Her face softened. "You've been going to see my shows?"

"I've been keeping a friendly eye on you," he said gruffly. "Haven't you seen any of the things *I've* done?"

"All of them. But it didn't involve going hundreds of miles to the back of beyond to sit in half-empty fleapits," she said, touched.

He shrugged. "What else are friends for?"

"But why did you never tell me?"

"Because I know how defensive you can become. You'd have gotten the idea that I was being kind or something, and then you'd have thrown a frying pan at me."

"Am I that bad?" she asked meekly.

His lips twitched. "You could be. You used to remind me of Napoleon, tiny and fierce."

They laughed and he continued, "I wouldn't have agreed to have you on *The Merry War* if I hadn't known your work and admired it."

"Is that really so? It wasn't... I mean, you weren't...?"

"I wasn't being kind. I never am where my work's concerned, and that's something I need to talk with you about." He took a deep breath, as though bracing himself, and said, "The fact is, Toni, after rehearsing with you for a week I have to say that things aren't working out quite as I expected."

Four

Nothing in Toni's whole life had been as bad as this moment. Flynn was telling her that she'd let him down. She swallowed hard and forced herself to speak calmly. "We're at a very early stage. You can't really see how a production's going to be—"

"Of course. I'm not talking about the production. I'm talking about me, an actor who badly needs your help, and who isn't getting much." He saw her face and immediately took her hand again. "Toni, don't look like that. We can put it right. It's just that you're so busy mother-henning Carole that you're not giving me any real direction."

Whatever she'd expected, it wasn't this. "But you're doing fine. You had the basics of a good performance there at the very first read-through."

"That was only skin deep. I still don't know what kind of man you think Benedick is, and what you think's really happening between him and Beatrice."

"Flynn, I'm flabbergasted. I thought you liked doing things your own way with the minimum of direction. I've heard you rail against heavy-handed directors."

"Sure you have, but that doesn't mean I want to be left rudderless. Give me strong direction now, then leave me alone to work out my own ideas that fit *your* overall scheme." He grinned suddenly. "I never thought I'd be complaining that you weren't telling me what to do. Remember the squabbles we had because you always read my scripts and were full of ideas about how I ought to tackle them?"

"Yes, and you used to tell me to be quiet..."

"Only because it confused me when you said one thing and the director said another. But your remarks were often very shrewd and somehow your suggestions used to creep into my performances."

She gaped at him. "But why didn't you ever tell me?" she asked at last.

He shrugged. "I don't know. It's the kind of thing you don't see clearly until afterward."

"Yes, but... Oh, Flynn, it would have meant the world to me to know I'd helped you. You always seemed so—" she struggled for the words "—so on top of everything. I used to feel intimidated by the way it all came so easily to you."

"Easily? Me?" He was genuinely astounded. "If you only knew—" He broke off and gave an awkward laugh. "Which brings us back to where we started, doesn't it? Perhaps I didn't really want you to know.

You were so bright-eyed about the theater and I suppose I wanted to keep it that way.''

She smiled. ''It wasn't only the theater I was bright-eyed about,'' she reminded him.

''Yes, well—'' Flynn looked embarrassed ''—I was young enough to enjoy showing off to you, playing the big man who could do it all on his own. Letting you know you were doing some of it for me would have spoiled it.'' He made a wry face. ''Pretty childish, huh?''

''I suppose we were both children.'' She brooded. ''We knew nothing about love, or each other. We just played with our shiny toys until we broke them.''

Abruptly she fell silent. She'd resolved a long time ago never to indulge in regrets. Only heartbreak lay in that direction. She looked up and found Flynn watching her. They both smiled uneasily, as if they'd caught each other off guard.

''Anyway,'' Flynn said in a slightly bemused voice, as though he were coming out of a dream, ''it's backfired on me now. You think I can work alone, and I can't. So tell me, how does it all look to you, Toni?''

''I think,'' she said slowly, ''that Benedick must have wooed Beatrice some time in the past, but he was only dallying. She found out and felt betrayed, because she was in deadly earnest. She says he once 'leant' her his heart for a while, 'and I gave him use for it,''' Toni quoted, ''''a double heart for his single one. Marry, once before he won it off me with false dice.'

''Now she keeps up a stream of witty abuse aimed at men in general, and Benedick in particular, to hide the fact that she still loves him.'' She saw Flynn frowning and said, ''You don't agree?''

"I agree there was something between them before, but he wasn't playing. He was deeply in love for the first time, and for a man that can be frightening. He felt the net closing in on him, lost his head and backed off clumsily." Flynn fell silent, studying the table as though it could inspire him.

"How?" Toni encouraged him after a moment.

"Perhaps he flirted a bit, to convince himself that he was still safe." Flynn gave a wry laugh that mocked the entire male sex, and added, "Of course, when you start reassuring yourself that you've seen the danger in time, it's already too late. He'd blunder on, making mistake after mistake, hurting her without meaning to, and never finding the courage to face his feelings and tell her about them."

Flynn lined up the salt, pepper and cheese pots in a perfect line, changed his mind and returned them to their original positions. He wasn't looking at Toni. "There's no end to the foolishness a man will commit when a woman means more to him than he can cope with," he said quietly. "To her, of course, it looks like cruelty. How's she to know the poor mutt is floundering around, calling to her for help because he's going down for the third time?"

"Perhaps if she was anything of a woman she'd know it by instinct," Toni ventured.

"You'd think so, but sometimes a woman, too, can be a bit dense about love. She doesn't realize what she has because he doesn't spell it out. She's listening to what he says, when she should be watching for the silent signals. If only she—"

Flynn broke off suddenly and gave an awkward laugh. When he resumed talking, the strange, intense note had been carefully wiped from his voice. "Even so, it was probably his fault. He swaggered around, pretending he could do without her. Why should any man expect a woman to see through that? She doesn't, of course, and puts too much emotional pressure on him, so he's completely out of his depth."

"But later they meet again, and now he knows his own heart, if only she'll give him a break. But she never stops ribbing him, so he ribs her back in self-defense. They've got another chance, but they have to learn how to take it."

"That would explain," Toni mused, "why he falls so easily for that trick his friends play on him. When he overhears them saying she's in love with him—"

"He's delighted," Flynn broke in eagerly. "He believes it because he wants so terribly to believe it. This man's desperate. He loves her but he knows he lost her through his own stupidity. That's the worst feeling in the world—to know that you once held your treasure *there*—" Flynn cupped his hands before him "—and you let it go because you were a fool." Slowly his hands relaxed and the fingers spread as if sand were running through them. He looked for a long time at the empty space, before saying softly, "Someone said that 'too late' are the saddest words in the world. They're also the most frightening. To come to your senses too late..." Flynn's voice trailed away and his face was bleak.

Toni had been holding her breath as she heard the pain and longing in Flynn's voice, and an incredible thought came to her. "Aren't you being a bit hard on him?" she asked cautiously. "It can't all be his fault. It wasn't very clever of her to put too much pressure on him too soon."

Flynn was still looking at his hands. "No, but I don't suppose she'd ever been seriously in love before, either," he said. "Unlike him, she wasn't afraid of her feelings, but she was inexperienced. If he'd been a bit wiser he'd have allowed for that. That's why they're ready for their second chance, because with maturity they may learn to understand each other."

"Yes," Toni whispered. "Yes . . ." Her heart was beating madly. "I wonder—" she hesitated, fearful of destroying this delicate moment by a clumsy word "—I wonder what they'd have done if their friends hadn't played that trick on them."

"They'd have found each other somehow," Flynn said simply. "People who really love each other always do."

She gave a shaky laugh. "It's so easy on the stage, isn't it? In real life there are no neat entrances and exits."

"Shall I refill your glasses, *signore*?"

The voice of the waiter made them look up quickly. They'd been leaning forward, heads almost touching as they spoke. Toni had a sensation of having come down to earth. As he talked to the waiter, Flynn's voice sounded normal and cheerful. There was no trace of the magic that had infused it a moment earlier. Or had it? Had she imagined the whole thing, believing what she wanted to believe?

In a flash the answer came to her. Flynn could slip so completely into another man's skin that he felt the character's emotions as his own. It was Benedick who'd spoken to her of love recaptured, in tones so heartfelt that briefly she'd become Beatrice, lost in the wonder of discovering she was still beloved.

But she wasn't Beatrice. She was sane, level-headed Toni Locksley, accustomed to Flynn's powers of illusion, and who should have known better than to hover on the brink of making a fool of herself. The laughter that emerged from her throat verged on hysteria.

"Toni?" Flynn stared at her, alarmed. "What on earth's the matter?"

"I'm sorry," she said, choking on her laughter. "It's really nothing that I can explain."

"You can't just go off into gales of laughter and say it's nothing."

"It would take too long," she said, recovering herself hastily and looking down at her food. "This looks delicious."

"You need it. You're wasting away."

"That's the strain of coping with my temperamental leading man," she said flippantly.

"I deny it. I obey you like a lamb. I've even asked you to boss me about some more."

"That's true," she said contritely. Having gotten him off the dangerous subject, she was prepared to admit anything.

They ate in silence for a few minutes. Toni's brow was furrowed, and Flynn, appreciating the intense mental activity that was going on inside, left her in peace. Now and then he glanced at her face. It wasn't conventionally pretty, but it was the face of an artist in the throes of creation, and as a fellow artist he found it beautiful at this moment.

Suddenly she stopped, fork in midair, and excited words tumbled from her as the pieces of the show began to fall into place in her brain. She talked without stopping for half an hour, while her food grew cold, oblivious to everything except the exhilarating birth taking place within her and the man sitting opposite. As she talked on, her words coming faster with the joy of discovery, she knew her excitement had communicated itself to Flynn. His eyes glowed with an understanding so perfect that his being seemed directly linked with hers.

Flynn watched her tenderly. In her eagerness she reminded him of the seventeen-year-old girl who'd ridden away with him on his motorbike with never a backward glance at her old life. She'd hated her dreary existence in that little town and had been overjoyed at finding someone to rescue her. He recalled how urgently she'd pleaded for him to take her back to London with him. He'd recognized the sound of the prisoner, ready to bargain anything for freedom, and it had given him an unfamiliar pain. Had she ever realized the danger of throwing in her lot with a stranger simply because he could offer escape?

He remembered her gratitude, so passionate that for a while it had been indistinguishable from love. But gratitude didn't last forever, and in the end she'd gone, as he'd known she would. Was that why he'd always protected a small part of himself from her, why, right to the end, he'd concealed the secret that tormented him?

It seemed an eternity since they'd talked together with such ease. The last months of their marriage had been a frozen wasteland of noncommunication, so bleak and arid that even their once-perfect physical harmony had died. He was still tortured by the memory of caressing her unresponsive flesh, seeing her eyes gaze desperately into his as they shared the terrible knowledge that there was an abyss between them.

"*That's* what's been wrong," Toni said triumphantly, as she finished. "I knew there was something. It'll need another duet for Beatrice and Benedick to make to clear. I'll talk to Duff and Joanna tomorrow." She pulled out a notebook and began writing.

"You'd better finish your dinner," Flynn said. "It's late and they want to close."

"I can't stop now," Toni said, scribbling madly. "I'll eat when I get home."

"Then let's go before we're thrown out."

While he was driving her home, Toni sighed happily and said, "Masks."

"I beg your pardon?" Flynn was startled.

"Masks, that's the secret. Beatrice and Benedick are each wearing masks, metaphorically speaking, and they have to drop them before they can 'see' each other. They even dance with each other at a masked ball..."

"Wearing real masks," Flynn supplied.

"That's it. Despite their masks each knows who the other is, and she knows that he knows. But *he* doesn't know that *she* knows. He thinks that she thinks she's talking to a stranger, but she knows she's talking to him. Am I confusing you?"

"Not in the least," Flynn said truthfully.

"She gets in a few digs at him. She's laughing up her sleeve at his discomfiture, but she's really unhappy, because she doesn't want to be making fun of him. She wants to be making love."

"There's the song!" they said together.

Toni leaned back in her seat, blissfully happy. The "something wrong" with the play that had eluded her till now had miraculously fallen into place. "I'll sleep well tonight for the first time since we started rehearsing," she sighed.

"Don't forget to eat. You left most of your food."

"Oh, sure," she murmured absently. "I'll just finish making my notes and then I'll put something together."

Flynn glanced quickly at her, but Toni was too sunk in thought to see the skeptical lift of his eyebrows. In another moment they'd reached her apartment and he followed her inside. "All right," he said briskly. "Sit down and get on with your notes. Leave everything to me."

"What are you doing?"

"Making sure you eat properly." Flynn was already filling the kettle.

"Flynn, it's sweet of you, but there's no need. I can manage."

"Sure you can, but you won't. If I go away you'll work till you drop and then crawl into bed starving. Go on with your notes."

She didn't argue any further, but sat down at the kitchen table and went on scribbling while he worked around her. In a short time he said, "All right," and she looked up to find the table laid and Flynn putting a plateful of scrambled eggs before her. "Eat," he commanded.

She took a few mouthfuls before thinking of something else to note down. Flynn made no protest, but calmly picked up the fork she'd dropped, piled it high with egg and said, "Open." She did so without taking her eyes off the page. She couldn't help but think how blissful it was to be looked after.

While he washed up Toni leaned back and stretched luxuriously. "Thank you," she said.

"My scrambled eggs are famous."

"No, I don't just mean the food. I mean for giving me the idea."

"But I didn't," he protested, turning quickly. "I provided the seed, that's all. You cultivated it into an idea. I couldn't have developed it as you just did."

"Well, I couldn't have done it without the seed."

Flynn shook his head. "All you needed was to talk to someone. I was just there, that's all."

"Thank you for being there," she insisted. "I don't know what I'd have done without you."

"Come on—" he hauled her to her feet "—time for you to go to bed. You've got to keep your strength up."

"No wait," she said, suddenly alert again. "There's just one more thing..."

"No, there isn't," he said. "Whatever it is will keep till tomorrow."

"But Flynn, listen to me—"

"Tomorrow! You're going to bed."

"Not till I've told you—"

"Peace." He laughed. "I will stop your mouth."

He lightly suited the action to the words, drawing her close and laying his mouth gently on hers. She was laughing, too, recognizing the quote, but at the touch of his lips the laughter died. Desire swept through her, invading her completely before she had time to think. There was a blaze of sweet fire and then it was too late.

She stood in his arms, rigid with shock, horrified by what she'd recklessly allowed to happen. Then everything was drowned in the sensations that had come to life with breathtaking urgency. She was trembling all over, already lost—beyond reason, beyond anything but this devastating awareness of him. Her body moved of its own accord to seek his. As he felt the pressure of her slim form molding itself against his length he slid one arm around her waist, drawing her into even more intimate contact. He placed his other hand at the back of her neck, working his fingers instinctively in the caresses he remembered she loved. That gentle stroking almost sent her out of her mind.

He'd kissed her only a few weeks ago, but it had been nothing like this. Her response then had been partly a jolt of surprise, partly an echo of a past that was gone. She'd controlled it and freed herself from him. But this headlong torrent of passion had raged out of control in the first second. Tonight their minds had met again. The channels of communication, so long silted over by estrangement, had miraculously cleared and the old desire had burst through, sweeping them both away in its flood.

He teased her with his lips, moving them lightly over her face, and her senses were reeling from the skillful sensuality of those kisses. Her response was to reach out eager hands and begin to trace the contours of his lean, hard frame.

"Flynn," she whispered. Then her voice became lost in a soft moan as Flynn covered her mouth again and his tongue found the sensitive flesh inside, moving against it in sensuous exploration. Immediately her tongue surged to meet his, challenging and caressing it.

A thousand remembered feelings coursed through her body. The mounting excitement of these mutual explorations had been their delight, and everything he was doing was evoking those dangerous sensations, full of poignant memories. The flickering movements of his tongue were an irresistible temptation, reminding her how long her starved senses had slept. Now Flynn's kiss had awakened them to new life, and there was no going back.

Without taking his mouth from hers Flynn had started to explore her. His hands traced her slim shape, and a growl of pure pleasure broke from deep in his throat as he rediscovered his favorite places. "Sweet," he whispered against her mouth, "sweet as you always were."

A soft sound of contentment was her only answer. It seemed to fire him on, for he scooped her up in his arms and carried her into the bedroom, kicking open the door. Once inside he sat down on the bed with Toni in his lap, and tore his mouth free long enough to say, "That's better. It was always awkward being a foot taller."

She gave a throaty chuckle that almost destroyed the last of his control. "You used to get an ache in your back, and I got a crick in my neck, d'you remember?"

"I remember, sweetheart. I remember everything about you, including the way you—what are you doing?"

"You used to like it. Don't you anymore?"

"Oh, yes," he said raggedly. "I like it as much as ever. I'd just forgotten what it felt like."

"Well," she murmured, "I'm reminding you." She looked up at him, blue eyes wide with assumed innocence, and he drew a sharp breath. "I'll stop if you like," she offered.

"Don't you dare. Just go on reminding me."

Toni obeyed the injunction, letting her hand roam at will beneath his shirt, which she'd torn open. His chest was smooth, and she could feel the tension directly against her palm. The knowledge that she'd raised a fever in this exciting male body thrilled her, and she began to rain soft teasing kisses on his neck. She paid particular attention to the places just below his ears where she knew he was especially sensitive. The sudden tightening of his arms, as if a jolt of electricity had gone through him, told her he hadn't changed.

She sighed with pleasure and extended her search around his body. The muscles of his back were taut with the effort of holding himself in check, and when she looked up into his eyes they were gleaming. She pulled his head down to hers and a groan broke from him at her skilled witchery.

When she freed his mouth Flynn looked down at her as if trying to see into her depths. She could read in his face everything she knew must be plain in her own: shock, bewilderment, fear, delight, and overmastering desire. "My god, how did this happen?" he asked hoarsely. "I didn't mean...I thought I had everything under control."

"Me, too," she said, trying to speak through the catch in her throat. "I guess we've been fooling ourselves."

"Or trying to," he whispered against her mouth.

He twisted his body suddenly, jerking backward and pulling her around so that she fell on the bed beside him. At once he started to work on the buttons of her shirt and she helped him eagerly. She couldn't wait to discard her boyish clothes so that he could discover beneath them a woman's body, ripe and flowering with desire for him.

He quickly dealt with the clasp of her front-hooked bra and pushed the material aside. She longed for him to kiss her breasts, but he stayed a moment, looking down at her as though mesmerized. His gaze seared her like the fiercest caress, and she felt the soft skin grow unbearably sensitive, waiting for him. She drew in a long, ragged breath as the feeling of burning anticipation began to spread outward from her taut nipples, down toward her stomach, and still farther down until it filled her loins.

"Flynn," she whispered.

At the urgent need in her voice he gave a slow smile, brilliant with promise, and the pounding in her blood grew faster and more heated. She moaned as he took her breasts in his palms. His touch on her fevered flesh was another brand added to the fire already raging within her, and she arched her body against his hands, silently pleading for the caresses she'd once known and loved. She knew now that she'd never forgotten them, never for a moment stopped yearning for them in all the lonely time apart.

He read the message in her trembling body and began to stroke her nipples softly with his thumb. Ecstasy pierced her again and again, mounting as his movements grew firmer and more purposeful. He looked down into her face, his own filled with delight at the proof of the miracle he was bringing about in her. "It wasn't too late after all," he said softly.

"Too...late?" she managed to whisper.

"For us," he said, dropping his head to one peaked, rosy nipple. His lips and tongue took up the work of his fingers, freeing his hand to slide lower and feel for the fastening of her jeans.

Toni lay suddenly still, as if a death knell had tolled in her head. "Too late...not too late." He'd spoken those same words earlier tonight, but he'd been talking about another couple, who only existed in his mind. Alarm stabbed at her. She knew Flynn's mind and the people who lived in it. Sometimes they had a terrible reality....

She tried to thrust the thought aside, but it pressed on her insistently. Flynn was a brilliant actor, who immersed himself in his roles and slipped in and out of them so easily that he could cross the boundary without knowing it. He'd kissed her with Benedick's words on his lips, and now she didn't know which man was making love to her. Was he Flynn, or was he Benedick? Could even he be sure at this moment? When he looked at her, whom did he see? Dismayed, she realized that he hadn't once spoken her name.

She desperately fought off the fears that hammered at her, but it *was* too late. Her body had sensed the dulling of her mind, and the new, vibrant life was dying out of it. Even as she fought to hold on to the moment, her flesh grew cold.

Flynn felt it at once. As her response faded his arms emptied of the joy that had filled them, leaving him holding a form that was dull and inert. He looked into her eyes and saw the stony, alien look that he dreaded. He'd seen it before in the last days of their marriage when they'd both been struggling to believe that everything wasn't over. "Where have you gone?" he asked desperately. "What happened?"

She couldn't answer. Dumb with misery she looked up at him before writhing out of his arms and burying her face in the bedspread. Flynn stretched out a hand to touch her, but stopped and drew it back. His eyes were full of shock. "I guess . . . this wasn't a very good idea after all," he said. He rolled off the bed and sat with his back to her, his head in his hands. He was trembling.

Toni drew herself up. "No," she said bleakly. Horrified, she looked down at her bare breasts, gleaming palely in the half-light. They throbbed with thwarted longing, and she scrambled off the bed and hastened to cover them.

Flynn had also risen to his feet. They dressed without looking at each other. When they'd finished, Toni managed to force a laugh. "I almost forgot my golden rule: never get involved with my leading man."

"How lucky you remembered in time," he said ironically but his voice was strained.

"It's a good rule, Flynn. Can we please pretend this never happened?"

"That's going to take a helluva lot of pretending." Flynn spoke lightly but his face was very pale.

"Well, you're good at that," she said, still determinedly smiling. "You told me once that you did your acting by believing. You said that if you believed in something enough it became true, and then it made you different. All you have to do is play the part of an actor who sees the director as *only* a director. That's what you've been, often enough."

"True. But an aspect of yourself is the hardest role in the world to play. You never quite know... No matter." He seemed to pull himself together. With an effort he stood up, went out to the kitchen and began gathering his things. Toni followed him.

"Thank you for everything you did for me tonight, Flynn. I mean it."

He didn't answer directly, but he turned at the door, looked her over for a moment and said, "Alec Wrighton must really be something."

He went out without waiting for an answer. She heard his footsteps climbing the steps, then the car starting up, and finally the sound of the engine fading to nothing.

Five

The next morning Toni held a meeting of the production staff to explain the "masks" theme that would dominate the show. As she talked she could sense the tension in her audience begin to relax. "We'll build up the masked ball, make it more central," she said. "Theo, the masks you've designed are lovely but—"

"But for what you're planning now, they've got to be different," Theo said, who was scribbling on his drawing pad. "No problem. I can see it already."

Then she turned to Duff and Joanna, explaining the new song that she wanted. They, too, were jotting down ideas. Toni looked around her, sensing the almost tangible relief that pervaded everyone now that their director had come up with the missing "something." "Has anyone got anything to add?" she asked.

"I think we could afford to make this idea a little more all-pervasive," Theo said. "It's not just Beatrice and Benedick who are hiding their true selves, is it? There's Don John who pretends to be a reformed character when he's actually the villain—"

Ellis picked up the theme. Joanna tossed in a thought. Someone else broke in on her, then another voice chimed in. Relief and happiness spread through Toni. Things were coming alive at last, and she owed this to Flynn.

She hadn't seen him yet that day, and she was wondering how they'd meet. She'd lain awake a long time after he'd left the night before, trying to talk herself into a sensible view of what had happened between them.

It would be foolish, she reasoned, to attach any importance to a momentary aberration. Last night Flynn had helped her as a friend, and because she was tired she'd overreacted. Her emotion had inspired him to "become" Benedick, and he'd gotten carried away, sweeping her along with him. The beating of her heart when he'd hinted at a second chance for them, and the physical rapture she'd known in his arms meant nothing. She'd been Beatrice responding to Benedick. It was the measure of Flynn's greatness as an actor that he could make that happen.

She didn't blame him. He was an impulsive, warm-hearted man who sometimes got more involved in the illusion than he meant to. In the cold light of day she knew he must be as relieved as she was that they'd stopped in time.

Luckily he thought it was Alec who'd stood between them. It should have been, Toni realized guiltily. But Alec hadn't been in her thoughts for a moment.

At rehearsal after lunch Flynn greeted her with an impersonally polite smile. She drew in her breath, bracing herself against the disappointment that rushed over her without warning and cursed herself as a fool.

"I want to take up where we left off yesterday afternoon," she said. "I've made some changes in that scene. Benedick, when you turn to Beatrice and say 'Peace, I will stop your mouth,' I want you to..."

She was punishing herself for her own stupidity, forcing herself to watch him with another woman in his arms, till repetition dulled the pain and dispelled the illusion of last night.

But something was the matter with Flynn. He seemed ill at ease and he muffed the embrace several times, each time growing more impatient with himself. "Look," he said at last in an edgy voice, "can you give me a break on this one, Toni? I'll get it right, I promise. But not today, okay?"

"Okay," she said in a carefully blank voice. "Ten minutes for coffee, then we'll take the start of Act Two."

She sat still a moment, staring blindly at her script, heedless of the movement around her, until she heard Gary's voice: "Hey, what's up?"

She started. "Gary! I didn't know you were there."

"I know. You were miles away, smiling to yourself as if someone had given you a present. Why so happy all of a sudden?"

For a mad moment Toni was tempted to tell him that she was rejoicing because her leading man had just given the worst performance of his life. Then sanity prevailed and she shook her head dumbly.

Gary held up his hand in a dramatic gesture. "Don't tell me..."

"I wasn't going to," she assured him.

"It's love, that's what it is. You can always tell when a woman's in love."

"Don't be ridiculous," she snapped. Then she recovered herself hastily and said in a cheerful voice, "Aren't you a bit young to be pontificating about women?"

"Women in love are the same the world over," he caroled.

"You don't say?" Flynn said, coming up behind him. "Tell us about it."

"Don't encourage him," Toni begged.

"I was saying it's as plain as day that Cupid has struck," Gary pronounced. "She was sitting there lost in a happy dream of the man she loves."

"Indeed?" Flynn's voice was pleasant enough, but it held a hint of warning.

"It's the mystery man, isn't it?" Gary asked, oblivious to any undercurrents. "You've gotten engaged. Oh . . . ah . . . yes—" his face changed with comic suddenness as he remembered that he was talking to Toni's husband "—you did say you two were just good friends."

"Gary, what are you twittering on about?" Toni asked. "What mystery man?"

"Your secret escort, the one you've been seen wining and dining with. Supposed to be in his forties, hair going gray at the sides, wears glasses . . . and nobody knows his name, including me."

"Let's keep it that way," said Toni with a shudder, imagining the look on Alec's face if he'd heard this conversation.

"Is there much talk?" Flynn asked.

"Well, naturally. Everyone wants to know how *you* feel, for a start."

Flynn appeared to considered this. "You mean in my role as rejected husband? Am I weeping into my pillow every night because my wife is madly in love with another man?"

Gary's eyes lit up and he began to scribble, murmuring, "Madly in love . . ."

"Cut it out, Gary," Toni said tensely.

"But you can't silence press speculation by refusing to talk," Flynn objected.

She bounded up in her seat. "Flynn, if you dare give an interview—" she threatened.

"Steady, now." Flynn took hold of her clenched fist. "Don't do it, pet. 'Director slugs leading man' is a great headline, but let's save it for closer to opening night. Besides—" he grinned suddenly in self-mockery "—ask Shep what my profile is costing him. He'll tell you to take care of it." He pushed her gently back into her seat, but kept hold of her fist for safety. "I wasn't thinking of an interview. Your gentleman friend and I should have a drink together, then everyone can see we get along fine."

"Hey, that's a great idea—"

"Forget it, Gary. Flynn, have you taken leave of your senses?"

"You don't think it's a good idea?" he inquired innocently.

"Certainly not! Gary, you'll just have to tell any journalists who ask that you don't know anything."

"Can't I even say that you're engaged?"

"You can say nothing at all!" Toni said furiously. She gathered her things and walked out before there could be any more questions. She needed to be alone to think. She'd been overjoyed by Flynn's uncharacteristic clumsiness that morning, but now her own reaction and its implications had horrified her.

If I'm not careful, she thought, I could imagine myself in love with him all over again. At least I saw the danger in time.

Over the next few days she tried to push Flynn out of her mind except as her leading man, but everything conspired against her. What had happened couldn't be undone. She'd lain in Flynn's arms, fevered with the passion that only he had ever incited in her. She'd felt the hard warmth of his body close to hers and known the longing to rediscover it. In another moment she knew she'd have stripped his clothes from him and discovered the answer to the questions that tormented her. Had he changed as a lover? Was he the same strong and fiery man who had brought her to ecstasy so often in the past?

She found herself studying him during rehearsals—not with the impersonal eyes of a director, but with the sensuous pleasure of a woman who desired him. Like everyone in the company, Flynn worked in a pair of threadbare jeans and a sweatshirt. It had never occurred to Toni before that this garb was provocative, but Flynn's clothes emphasized the lithe masculinity of his movements in a way that had her longing to remove them.

Things were no better when the company began to rehearse in makeshift costumes so that the actors could get used to moving in unfamiliar garments. Flynn appeared in a pair of black tights and a loose shirt that fell open halfway down, revealing a smooth, tanned chest. The sight reminded her of how she'd lain against that chest, listening to the pounding of his heart and touching the warm flesh that responded so vibrantly to her caresses.

But gradually a new problem arose to occupy the front of her mind. Carole was improving fast. Duff and Joanna had provided the new song, which everyone agreed was a winncr. Theo had come up with some fresh designs for the masked ball and they were exactly right. Everything was going splendidly, yet Toni had a sinking feeling that the show was getting bogged down.

The old despair seized her again. It would have been a relief to talk to Flynn, but the memory of the last time was like a barrier between them. His manner toward her now was completely professional, even a little remote, and it dawned on Toni that for the first time since she'd know him, Flynn wasn't there for her to turn to—even as a friend. The thought washed over her in an aching wave of loneliness.

Alec was away for a few days. He called her when he returned and she felt a blessed sense of relief at the sound of his voice. Dear, solid, prosaic Alec would restore her sense of proportion. She gladly agreed to have dinner that night, but vetoed his suggestion of collecting her at the theater. Mercifully Flynn seemed to have forgotten his idea of meeting Alec, but she didn't want to risk an accidental encounter.

"There's a new restaurant I'd like to try," Alec said. "It's near the theater, so why don't we meet there? It's called Il Papagallo."

"That has a familiar ring."

"I believe it has a very good reputation. I'll see you there at eight o'clock," he said, after giving her the address.

When she reached Il Papagallo that evening, she knew why the name had rung a bell. This was where Flynn had brought her a week ago. After a moment she shrugged. There was no reason why she shouldn't come here with Alec as well.

The restaurant was lit entirely by candles, but at last she made out Alec waiting at a table in the dim light. She hurried to him and impulsively she blurted out, "Oh Alec, I'm so glad to see you."

"Darling," he looked startled by her fervent tone, but didn't seem to catch the desperation in her voice. He leaned forward slightly and for a moment she thought he'd kiss her. But he checked himself and looked around self-consciously.

"Risk it," she urged him teasingly. "No one will see."

But he contented himself with squeezing her hand. Toni felt a rush of tenderness for him. He might be conventional and unimaginative, but he was as steady as a rock and she always knew exactly where she was with him. After the past few weeks, that suddenly seemed the most attractive quality in the world.

Gino, the proprietor, appeared. *"Signore,"* he said, "I have a favor to ask you. Your waiter tonight will be my nephew Mario. He has arrived from Italy only a few days ago, and his English is very bad. He's a good boy and he tries hard, but if you can be patient with him..." Gino made an expressive gesture.

"Naturally we'll make allowances," Alec said graciously.

"*Grazie, signore.* I send Mario to you." Gino bustled away.

"It seems like an age since I saw you," Alec said, taking hold of her hand.

"Signore." They both turned at the anxious voice that announced Mario's arrival. He was a gangly, unattractive youth, with hunched shoulders and a halfhearted moustache. He wore a pair of round steel-rimmed spectacles that gave him the look of a flustered owl. "I am appeared," he announced unnecessarily.

"Good," Alec said, raising his voice a decibel.

"You are drunken," Mario declared.

"Pardon?" Alec looked at him, startled.

"You are drunken," Mario repeated eagerly. "What have I got you?"

"You haven't gotten us anything yet," Alec said patiently.

"No, *signore*. I wait for you to ask to be drunken."

"I think he's asking what we want to drink," Toni said chuckling.

"Si, si, signorina. Grazie, grazie!" Overwhelmed with gratitude the young man seized Toni's hand and kissed it.

"We don't do that in England," Alec said sharply.

"Pardon, signore?" Mario's brow was furrowed with anxiety, and he leaned toward Alec, so eager to learn that he seemed not to know he was still holding Toni's hand.

Alec raised his voice again and spoke slowly. "I said we—don't—do—that—in—England." Then, as Mario still didn't let go, Alec repeated, "Not—do—in—England." He sighed in exasperation. "Let go! *Down!*"

"Alec," Toni said under her breath, "you're talking to him as if he were a dog."

"He's a damned fool, if you ask me," Alec muttered.

"*Si, signore.* My mother say the same," Mario said, beaming.

Toni gave a small choke of laughter, and Alec frowned. "Don't encourage him, darling, and please make him let go of your hand. People are looking at us."

"May I have my hand back please?" Toni said, smiling up at the young waiter.

This time he seemed to understand, for he smiled back and released her at once. She had only a fleeting glimpse of his face before he turned toward Alec, but something about it gave her a shudder of alarm.

"Now, *signore*, I get you drunken," Mario offered.

Alec sighed and gave the order in a slow, loud voice that suggested he was talking to a half-wit, and Mario sped away. Toni watched him go, wishing the restaurant was better lit. She'd had a vague impression of Mario's height, moustache and glasses, but that was all.

I've got to stop imagining things, she reproved herself. I'm beginning to see Flynn everywhere.

"What's been happening while I've been gone?" Alec asked.

"I've been working night and day."

"Don't work too hard, will you? There's no sense in exhausting yourself."

"But you have to exhaust yourself if you're trying to create something," she said earnestly.

"I only meant that I'm concerned for your health. Have you missed me at all?"

"Oh, yes," she said fervently. "There've been so many times when I've thought, if only Alec were here..."

Mario interrupted them with their order. As he served their drinks Toni tried to get a better view of his face, but he never looked directly at her. At last he gave a menu to each of them and said brightly, "Now you must order me."

Alec dealt with the ordering by pointing at items on the menu, thus leaving the waiter little scope for confusion. Mario made copious notes and departed. Alec smiled at Toni. "I thought you seemed a bit tense when I— Toni, you're not listening to me. Why are you looking over there?"

"I was watching our waiter. He reminded me of someone, but I expect it's just my imagination. What were you saying?"

"I was saying you seemed a bit tense just before I left. Had anything gone wrong?"

"Oh, nothing specific. Things were just getting on top of me."

"Is your husband giving you trouble?"

Toni hesitated before saying in a constrained voice, "He works hard and he's a good actor. No director can ask for more."

"But he presumes on your relationship, doesn't he? I'm increasingly sorry I let you do this show."

"You didn't let me," Toni said indignantly. "I didn't ask your permission, Alec, and I didn't need it."

"Of course not. But you won't deny that you had some qualms on my account. In fact you were on the verge of turning it down."

"Yes, but . . ." Toni frowned, trying to remember what she'd said that night.

"I asked you if you were still in love with him, and you said you hadn't been for a long time."

A crash from behind them announced Mario's reappearance with their appetizers. He'd banged the tray down on a side table and now proceeded to serve from it laboriously. Alec went on talking. "You gave me the impression you never had been very much in love."

Toni lifted her head sharply. She made a gesture of instinctive protest and opened her mouth to rebut this but Alec went on, "You seemed to regard him as an adolescent infatuation that you'd outgrown."

Toni was uncomfortably aware of Mario standing by them, uncorking the wine. He seemed totally absorbed in his task, but there was no way of knowing whether he'd heard Alec's last words.

Alec tasted the wine Mario poured for him, nodded, and continued, "Do you know, that was the night I first began to hope that you really would marry me. You said you wanted someone quite different from Flynn Rawley, someone solid and reliable—" He stopped speaking and turned irritably to Mario who was hovering, bottle in hand.

"The wine, *signore*? Is okeydokey?"

"The wine is acceptable," Alec said frigidly. "Please serve the lady." He spoke with the natural testiness of a man who'd been interrupted in midproposal, and added, "This is the last time I come to this madhouse."

They sat in silence for a moment, while Toni watched Mario leave. "It's strange," she mused, "how distinctive someone's walk can be."

"I beg your pardon?"

"Almost as distinctive as their earlobes."

"Toni, you're not making sense."

Gathering her wits, she asked, "Alec, how did you come to choose this place?"

"Actually, it chose me. I received a voucher for a free meal for two people. It was waiting in my post when I got back to the office."

"And you called and reserved a table for tonight?"

"Yes. What is it, Toni?"

"Nothing. I just wondered, because you don't normally come to Italian restaurants."

"Well, I'll certainly never come to this one again. Do you mind if we drop the subject? I'd like to finish proposing to you. I have a funny feeling that tonight is the best chance I'll ever get."

She gave a wry smile. "You don't know how right you are," she said.

"Does that mean you'll marry me?"

"I suppose it does," she said lightly.

For a moment she thought he'd kiss her this time, but he merely smiled. Toni smiled back, relieved to have made the decision at last. When she was Alec's wife there'd be no more turmoil in her life.

"I've changed my mind," Alec said. "I'm glad you did the show after all. I said being around that man would send you into my arms, and it has."

"He's certainly made me appreciate you more," Toni agreed.

"Enough to make you give the whole thing up when this is over?"

"Give up?" She stared at him in disbelief. "You mean leave the theater completely?"

"Well, yes. You'll have had your little bit of success by then. Won't that satisfy you?" Then, as he read the answer in her eyes, he added hastily, "Let's leave that for later. This is a celebration. I'll order some champagne as soon as I see our waiter, although I suppose we'll be lucky if he doesn't kill us with the cork."

Mario appeared at that moment with a trolley bearing a small burner, as Toni had ordered a dish that needed to be flambéed at the table. "Now we're engaged," Alec continued, "we must try to get your divorce through as soon as possible." A suppressed shriek from the hapless Mario announced that he'd burned himself. "Oh, God," Alec muttered.

"Ignore him," Toni said firmly.

"How can I ignore him?" Alec said crossly. "Might as well try to ignore a gnat. At least with a gnat you can spray insect repellent, but how do you get rid of this idiot?"

"Non e vero, non e vero," yelped Mario. *"Non sono idiòta."* His voice grew tearful. "*Signorina, ti prègo,* I am meaning no harm. You find me appealing—"

"The hell she does," Alec growled.

"I think he means he's appealing to us," Toni said hastily.

"*Si, si*, I am very appealing. You are kind, *signorina*. You will plead for me with your papa."

Alec seemed about to explode. To her annoyance Toni felt her lips begin to twitch. She was furious with Flynn, of course, but in some perverse way the stunt was amusing. Over the flambé she tried to glare at him. Two dark eyes, gleaming with wicked humor, looked back, daring her to give him away.

It would have been a pleasure to do so, but she couldn't risk it. Alec's temper was rising to boiling point, and instinct warned her that if there was a scene, Flynn would come off best. Besides, there were other ways of putting him in his place. "Of course I'll intercede for you *with my fiancé*," she said sweetly. "But only if you get us a bottle of champagne. We've just become engaged and we want to celebrate."

He left, but not before giving her a look only she could decipher.

"Thank you, darling," Alec said through gritted teeth. "Where were we? Oh yes, your divorce. Can you hurry it up?"

"Flynn's in a funny mood," she said, speaking quickly in case Mario returned. "We were going to ask the court for a divorce by mutual consent, because we've been apart more than two years. But we have to both want it. I thought it was all agreed, but now he's talking about fighting it. Mind you, that's probably just one of his jokes."

"Haven't you got any other grounds?"

"Not a thing. I suppose he's had his romances since we split up, but if so he's been very discreet."

Mario had returned bearing a bottle of champagne and was struggling with it. Alec became lost in thought. "Toni, how long exactly have you two been separated?" he asked at last.

"Four-and-a-half years."

"Splendid! Then in six months you can divorce him whether he likes it or not."

She stared. "Without grounds?"

"You'll have grounds. Under English law you need his consent if you've only been apart two years, but if you've been apart for five it doesn't matter if he agrees or not. A court will free you from him automatically and he can't do a thing to stop it. Didn't you know that?"

Out of the corner of her eye Toni became aware that Mario's movements had stilled. "No, I didn't," she said slowly.

"I thought the two of you looked up the law ages ago."

"*He* looked up the law. He said the simplest thing would be to divorce by consent after two years apart. We agreed on that, so I didn't ask any further." She brooded for a moment, then looked up, realizing that Mario was ready with the champagne. She gave him a dazzling smile as he poured the foaming liquid into two glasses. "I've just had a wonderful idea," she said breathlessly. "I want to share this celebration with everyone—" her eyes gleamed at Mario, who glared balefully back "—even you!" she told him.

"Toni, what are you talking about?" Alec said, alarmed.

Toni held a glass of champagne out to Mario. "I want you to celebrate with us as a reminder of the most wonderful night of my life," she told him in an ecstatic voice.

"He probably doesn't understand a word you're saying," Alec growled.

"He understands perfectly," Toni assured him. "Don't you, Mario?" Her eyes glinted suddenly. She knew if she didn't pay Flynn back in his own coin tonight his ghost would haunt her marriage. She continued in a challenging voice, "You understand that tonight I'm more blissfully happy than I've ever been before, and you're delighted for me, aren't you?"

Mario's eyes met hers over the rim of the glass, and their look sent a shaft of pain through her. "No, *signorina,*" he said softly.

But the moment passed and he began blurting words out pell-mell. "*Si, si,* is much romantico. But *signore*—" Mario leaned to Alec in a confiding manner "—is no need to wait. You and the *signorina* must become lovers, and then the wicked husband make the divorcing damn quick. Or perhaps he shoot you, but I can tell you are man of great passion, who think the world well lost for love—"

But this was too much for Alec. Goaded past endurance he thumped the table for silence and in a terse voice demanded another waiter.

Mario tottered away in despair. Toni pressed her lips firmly together to control a wild desire to laugh. When she could trust herself to speak again she said, "There is always that way, of course."

"What way?"

"We could live together openly, and then Flynn would be glad to get rid of me."

"Toni, I don't know what's come over you tonight. You must know quite well that's out of the question."

Toni regarded him, her head on one side. If Alec had been perceptive he might have been disturbed by the steely glint in her eyes. "Why is it?" she demanded. "I thought you wanted to marry me as soon as possible. This way you can."

"I do want to marry you as soon as it's reasonably possible—"

"So you don't think the world's well lost for love?"

"Please, my dear, is there any need to talk in that melodramatic fashion? We're civilized adults."

The sounds of a violent altercation erupted from the kitchen. The door was flung open and Gino stormed out and approached their table. Mario trotted after him and hovered tearfully in the background as Gino poured out his apologies. "*Mi scusi signore*, I should not have asked you to endure this *cretino di cretini*."

"All right, all right," Alec said irritably. "If we could just have another waiter—"

"But of course, *signore. Maria vergine*, I cannot forgive myself for inflicting such an object on you, but he is my sister's boy, you understand, and I promised to give him a chance although I knew he was a little..." Gino touched his forehead significantly.

"Of course, now if we could just—"

"But for a customer such as yourself, I forget even my promise to my sister. He is fired."

Mario set up a wail of anguish and Gino turned on him. "Enough!" he said fiercely. "You have disgraced me. *Go!*"

"No...no, look, that's not necessary," Alec said uncomfortably.

"Alec," Toni said in an urgent voice.

"Please, my dear, just be quiet for a moment while I deal with the situation."

"But there's no need," she said frantically.

"I think I'm the best judge of that. I didn't mean to get the boy fired even if he is a fool." Alec raised his voice, trying to be heard above Gino's raging and Mario's tearful pleas. "I'm sure he means well," he roared. "Don't fire him, just get me another waiter."

Nobody seemed to be taking any notice of him so he took a deep breath to try again. Toni groaned, knowing there was no help for it. "Alec," she shouted above the din. "You don't have to worry about him. *It's Flynn.*"

"Toni, will you please—what did you say?"

"I said that waiter is Flynn."

The word was like a magic charm, stilling the commotion in a second. In the silence that followed, Flynn removed his spectacles and tore off the little moustache. He grinned at Alec. Gino melted tactfully away.

Alec had half risen in his seat. Now he fell back. "That," he said, hoarsely, "is Flynn Rawley, your husband?"

"Yes, I'm afraid so."

He was wide-eyed with outrage. "Do you mean to sit there and tell me that this whole thing has been a put-up job between you?"

"Of course not," she said quickly. "I had no idea what was going to happen. You chose this place."

"I was set up to choose it, wasn't I?"

"Yes, I'm afraid you were," Toni said. "But not by me." She glared at Flynn. "I promise you, Alec, I'm going to make him sorry for this."

Alec was staring at her. "But when you saw him you didn't tell me."

"I didn't recognize him at first."

"Do you expect me to believe you didn't know your own husband?"

"It's very dark in here," she pleaded.

"Besides, Toni doesn't lie," Flynn said quietly. "If you're in love with her you should know that."

"Stay out of this!" Alec snapped. He began to gather his things together. "I don't think we have anything more to say to each other, Toni. I don't know when I've been as disappointed in anyone as I am in you."

"Alec, I give you my word that I had nothing to do with this. I only became sure it was Flynn a few minutes ago, and then I thought it would be more tactful to say nothing. You don't really think I'm lying, do you?"

"What I think," he said stiffly, "is that the two of you are birds of a feather. Please don't try to come with

Say YES to free gifts worth over $20.00

Say YES to a rendezvous with romance, and you'll get 4 classic love stories—FREE! You'll get an LCD digital quartz watch—FREE! You'll get a stylish ballpoint pen—FREE! And you'll get a delightful surprise—FREE! These gifts carry a value of over $20.00—but you can have them without spending even a penny!

MONEY-SAVING HOME DELIVERY

Say YES to Silhouette and you'll enjoy the convenience of previewing 6 brand-new books delivered right to your home every month. Each book is yours for only $2.24 – 26¢ less than the retail price, and there is no extra charge for postage and handling.

SPECIAL EXTRAS—FREE!

You'll get our monthly newsletter, packed with news of your favorite authors and upcoming books—FREE! You'll also get additional free gifts from time to time as a token of our appreciation for being a home subscriber.

Say YES to a Silhouette love affair. Complete, detach and mail your Free Offer Card today!

YOUR "NO RISK GUARANTEE"

- There's no obligation to buy—and the free books and gifts are yours to keep forever.
- You receive books before they're available in stores.
- You may end your subscription anytime—just write and let us know.

If offer card is missing, write to: Silhouette Books
901 Fuhrmann Blvd., P.O. Box 9013, Buffalo, NY 14240-9013

DETACH AND MAIL CARD TODAY

NO POSTAGE
NECESSARY
IF MAILED
IN THE
UNITED STATES

BUSINESS REPLY CARD

First Class Permit No. 717 Buffalo, NY

Postage will be paid by addressee

Silhouette Books®
901 Fuhrmann Blvd.
P.O. Box 9013
Buffalo, NY 14240-9963

me. I'd rather not drive you home, and I've no doubt you'll get another offer. Good night."

Dismayed, Toni watched Alec shoulder his way out of the restaurant. It was the first time she'd ever seen him lose his temper and she was torn between indignation and pity. She looked askance at Flynn who'd slid into the vacant seat. Smiling, he filled a glass and held it out to her.

"Have some champagne," he said.

Six

Birds of a feather! Fancy him insulting me by likening me to you!'' She looked at Flynn, regarding her with a mocking, unrepentant grin, and added in exasperation, ''If you really were a bird I'd buy an air gun! Of all the unscrupulous . . .''

He laughed. ''You should have let me meet him, then I wouldn't have had to be drastic. Luckily Gino's a good friend and agreed to help. The hardest part was tracking Wrighton down, but I knew he was a stockbroker, and his name's on his firm. I had a voucher printed, Gino called me as soon as the reservation turned up, and I hurried along. Don't scowl at me, darling. You ought to be thanking me for saving you from a terrible mistake.''

''I'll thank you to stop interfering in my life. It's no concern of yours who I marry.''

''It is as long as you're still married to me.''

"Well, that won't be long."

"It'll be as long as I can make it. You can't marry Wrighton. He brings out the worst in you. Really, Toni, what do you see in him?"

"I know where I am with Alec."

Flynn raised a cynical eyebrow. "Is that the best you can say of a man you're supposed to be in love with?"

"It's a very great deal," she said firmly.

"After me, you mean?" He grimaced. "Was I really such a monster that that pompous stuffed shirt looks good in comparison?"

"No, you weren't a monster, Flynn. I didn't know what you were. It was like living with a dozen men, and no way of knowing which was the real one. You were always so clever at being someone else, but I needed you to be you. At least Alec is solid, he's *there.*" Her voice finished on a ragged note.

"The point, my darling, is that he *isn't* there. He walked out on you because you committed the crime of getting him stared at in a public place. He's solid enough, I grant you. So's a brick wall or a suet pudding, but you don't turn to them in a crisis. Where was Alec Wrighton last week when you needed some help and understanding?"

She was silent, trying to find an answer, knowing there wasn't any. At last Flynn added gently, "And I seem to remember that we had some good times." His eyes met hers, silently evoking the blissful harmony of the flesh that had once been theirs. Vibrant, living memories awoke within her, and she felt the heat begin to steal over her body. She was glad now of the poor light so that Flynn couldn't see the reaction in her face.

"Yes, we had some good times," she said abruptly. "Let's remember those and forget the rest."

"But I don't want to forget any part of our marriage," he said softly. "Even the bad things left something valuable behind."

She couldn't suppress the anger she felt at the easy way he could call up painful feelings that she longed to forget, and put her at war with herself. Fear made her cruel. "I can believe it. Nothing was ever wasted with you, was it? It all turned up in some role or other, eventually. I'm glad I was useful."

She heard the sharp intake of his breath and was instantly sorry, but before she could say so Flynn had replied coolly, "You were very useful, but then so was I, wasn't I? Every woman should have one adolescent infatuation in her life, if only to get the nuisance out of the way."

"Flynn..."

"Shall we go, or do you want to finish your dinner?"

"No, I don't want anything. Flynn I didn't mean..."

"Toni, let's not start explaining to each other what we meant," he said tiredly. "Our worst arguments always began that way."

They drove home in silence. Toni was appalled at the pain she'd heard in Flynn's voice as he repeated Alec's contemptuous dismissal of their love. She longed to comfort him but he'd retired behind a barrier of courtesy. It was unlike him to be aloof, and she realized that once again he'd become a stranger. She was paralyzed by the same feeling of helplessness that had afflicted her in the old days whenever his personality had undergone these disconcerting changes.

When they drew up outside her door she tried again to tell him she was sorry. "No, I'm sorry," he said quietly. I guess I have a lot to apologize to you for, in particular for making you so unhappy that Alec Wrighton looked like a good alternative. I hadn't realized..."

"Listen to me," she begged. "I never told Alec that you were an adolescent infatuation. They're his words. Please, Flynn, you must believe me."

"All right, I believe you. Besides, it's all academic now."

"No, it isn't,'" she said passionately. "We had something that was beautiful. I want us both to remember it that way, not spoil the memories by misunderstandings."

"You're right," he said. "We won't say any more." He smiled at her, cheerful and friendly again, but the smile was like a hastily donned mask. With a feeling of despair she knew she hadn't gotten through to him. She wanted to try to say some of the million things that were in her heart, but already he was leaning across her to open the door. She got out, said "Good night" bleakly, and watched him drive away.

For the next week Toni was too sunk in work to pay much attention to the ache of sadness in her heart that wouldn't go away. Life in the Regent Theatre became more tense as opening night grew inexorably nearer. Carole's performance had suddenly taken off as Flynn had always predicted, and now Toni could see why he'd wanted her. They were an ideal couple, glowing in each other's light. It took all Toni's professionalism to watch them and be glad of their shared magic.

But despite the improvements, Toni was still haunted by the sense of something wrong, something she couldn't define.

One afternoon the production office of *Dead and Alive* called to say that the West End transfer had fallen through and the play was closing. When she returned to the stage she tried to force a smile but her stomach was knotted with tension. "Where were we?" she asked tiredly, as she slumped into her seat.

"Look," Flynn said, "why don't we give it a break for now? I don't just mean today, but for a couple of days."

"Take time off at this stage?" Toni couldn't believe she was hearing him correctly.

"It would be the best thing we could do. We're all worn out. A few days away from the show would give us some fresh life."

"All right," she said after a moment. "School's out, everyone! Be back on Monday."

There was a faint cheer. Toni hauled herself out of her chair, thankful that Flynn had given her the excuse to crawl away alone for a while. She went home to pack a bag, gave the key to her apartment to a neighbor and took a train to Kelby, a seaside resort on the north coast, where she'd spent happy holidays as a child. It was a desolate place in winter, and no one would find her.

She traveled by night sleeper and arrived in the early morning. She booked a room in the first hotel she found, and went straight out to walk along the seafront, which, as she'd hoped, was deserted. The sea was the color of slate except for the foam whipped up by the wind. She leaned into the gusts that tried to blow her backward and clutched her jacket around her.

The phone call had been the final straw on the burden of depression she now realized she'd been carrying since the incident in the restaurant. Flynn seemed to have withdrawn from her. Before the rest of the cast he was always friendly and courteous, but they hardly exchanged two words alone. The night when they'd almost found each other again might never have happened.

She wondered if he were with Carole now. He hadn't said he wasn't romancing her, Toni remembered; only that this wasn't why he wanted to act with her. She felt the ache in her heart grow stronger. With every fiber of her being she yearned for Flynn to be here with her so that she could tell him her troubles and have him laugh her back to sanity. "Birds of a feather," Alec had said, and foolishly she'd denied it. But there was no one she wanted as much as she wanted Flynn, no one else who understood.

What a fool I was, she thought bitterly. We were friends and I threw even that away. But in the same moment a flash of understanding came to her, forcing her to cast aside the illusion she'd clung to.

I don't want his friendship. I want much more. I want what I can never have again!

The wind buffeted her, making her eyes water. She passed a hand across her face, but the tears wouldn't stop. They ran down her cheeks and seemed to have something to do with the hard lump in her throat. Desolation shook her as she realized what she'd lost, and how completely it was gone. She clutched the sea rail, fighting to regain control of herself. It was too late for tears, too late for regrets. What had Flynn said about the words "too late" . . . ?

She turned and began to trudge back to the hotel. In the distance the tall figure of a man was coming toward her. Her eyes were still too blurred for her to make him out clearly, but she could see him raise an arm as if to hail her. Something in that movement made her stop in her tracks, staring frantically as the man waved again and began to run toward her. Then she was running, too, her heart bursting with joy as his arms opened to receive her. In another moment she was enfolded in the embrace she'd longed for.

She hugged him fiercely and felt him crush her in return. Then Flynn's hand was under her chin, raising her face for his kiss. His lips were warm and firm on hers, and she held him more tightly than ever, knowing she was in the one place in the world she wanted to be. If only he'd never let her go. But at last he released her and said, "Let's get under cover before we die of cold."

They found a small tea shop nearby and settled at a table by the window. Outside the wind howled and the sea was whipped to new frenzy, but Toni felt only the warmth of Flynn's presence.

He ordered tea and scones, then took her hand. "I heard about *Dead and Alive*," he said. "I'm sorry, Toni. But it isn't the end of the world. Plays come and go."

"Yes, I know. It just caught me at a bad moment."

"I guessed that was why you came from the phone looking so stricken. I thought you might feel like crying on a friend's shoulder. I was going to offer you mine but you vanished before I could talk to you. I drove all night after your neighbor told me you'd come here. I blamed myself that you ran away. If I hadn't acted like a jerk the other evening you'd have felt you could come to me, wouldn't you?"

"Is that why you came here?" she said. "Just to be friendly?"

"Just to be friendly. I think you need a friend very badly just now."

She nodded. Her mind had taken in the message, but disappointment was swallowed up in joy that he was here at all. He'd come searching for her, to give her the warmth and comfort he knew she needed.

"I've booked a room at a place called Clifftops. Where are you staying?" Flynn asked.

"The Strand Hotel."

"I'll get my things and join you."

He drove her back to the Strand. As she prepared to get out of the car he kissed her and said, "I'll be along in half an hour. Don't worry about anything. You've got me here to cheer you up now."

She spent the time in a fever of impatience. When the half hour passed she looked out of the window, peering down the street for his car, but there was no sign. When he still hadn't come after three-quarters of an hour she was convinced he'd had an accident. She paced the floor for a few more minutes, then went downstairs to reception, but stopped in her tracks at the scene there.

A tall man stood at the desk. His appearance was colorful, from the heavy overcoat that came down to his calves to the red hair, streaked with gray, that flowed out from beneath the brim of his hat and combined with a luxuriant beard. He was talking to the receptionist in a guttural accent and seemed to be having difficulty with his English.

Toni watched in delight. It was a clever impersonation and might have fooled her if she hadn't been so used to Flynn's variety of characters by now. Plus, of course, he'd virtually warned her what he was going to do when he spoke of cheering her up. She stayed where she was, enjoying the performance. The red-haired man and the receptionist had reached a stalemate of mutual incomprehension and were glaring at each other. "I insist," the man said in a loud voice, "you tell Herr Schneider I am arrived."

The receptionist took a deep breath and spoke even louder. "There is no Herr Schneider here," she declared.

The man hauled out a dictionary and flipped over the pages. "Conference!" he bellowed at last.

"There's no conference here, either," the receptionist said, trying to remain calm. "Wrong hotel."

Toni chuckled and the receptionist looked at her frantically. "What shall I do with him?" she demanded.

"Throw him out," Toni said. "He's obviously a dishonest vagabond." She noted with pleasure that the red-haired man seemed to understand this, for he glared at her.

"Do you think so," asked the receptionist doubtfully. "He says he's a Professor Hermann."

"Professor, nothing!" Toni said firmly. "If he's a professor I'm Mata Hari." She leaned over the desk and became confiding, "If you ask me, he's come to steal the silver. Look at that shifty face! I expect the beard comes off. Here, I'll show you."

She seized the beard and tugged hard. The man gave a yell of outrage and backed sharply away. Toni was dragged after him, her hand frozen to the beard, which hadn't budged. She swallowed nervously and gave another desperate tug. But despite the combined efforts of herself and her victim, whose jaw was working furiously on the other end, the beard stayed firmly in place. Then a sound made her look up, and her blood ran cold.

Flynn was standing in the doorway.

She stared at him, paralyzed with horror. The beard slipped out of her nerveless hand, and the man backed away and flattened himself against the wall. Toni's gaze was still riveted on Flynn, whose face was full of unholy delight. Her mouth was dry. "You . . ." she managed to croak. She pointed to the professor and said the only thing she could think of, "you should have been him."

"I'm sorry, darling," Flynn said meekly. "I didn't know you wanted me to be him, or I would have been." His eyes were dancing.

"Everything all right? I heard some screaming." Flynn stepped aside from the doorway to reveal a large, uniformed policeman. Professor Hermann hurled himself into the arms of the law and launched into an excited explanation, from which it emerged that he'd been attacked by brigands, hit over the head, robbed and left for dead. The policeman heard him out phlegmatically, cast his eyes over Toni's petite form, and asked, "This lady did all that, sir?"

With shrieks and gestures the professor gave him to understand that this was a madwoman with the strength of ten.

"I only pulled his beard," Toni said indignantly.

"I see, miss. And why would that be?"

"I thought he was my husband," she said, realizing at once that this didn't help.

"Do you make a habit of pulling your husband's beard, then?"

"Of course not. My husband doesn't have a beard."

This time the policeman just looked at her.

"I'm her husband," Flynn said helpfully.

The policeman turned his gaze on Flynn's youthful, clean-shaven form, then onto Professor Hermann. His face spoke volumes about anyone who could confuse the two. "Have you been celebrating Christmas a bit early, miss?" he enquired kindly. "A drop too much to keep out the cold, perhaps?"

Toni began to refute this indignantly, but Flynn's hand over her mouth silenced her. "Actually, the truth's rather sad, Officer," he said. "She's a bit, you know—" he nodded significantly "—I don't usually let her out on her own, but she gave me the slip this time." He ignored the furious sounds coming from behind his hand and hurried on smoothly, "If I could just take her home with me now, I promise you there'll be no more trouble."

"I think that might be best, sir."

"Yes, get her out of here," snapped the receptionist. "She'll give the place a bad name."

"Conference!" roared the unlucky professor.

"Just down the road, sir," the policeman informed him, "at the Inn On The Strand."

Toni held her tongue until she was seated beside Flynn in the car. Then she said in a voice that shook with mingled exasperation and amusement, "I'll never forgive you as long as I live."

He grinned. "Why, for implying that you had a screw loose? It was the only thing that saved you from a police cell. Or is it my fault for not being him?"

"Of course it is," she said indignantly. "You've always been 'him' in the past."

Flynn nodded, apparently following the logic of this. "Poor Toni," he said. Then he began to laugh. "If you could have seen your face. I wouldn't have missed it for anything in the world."

She joined in. They were still laughing when he drew up outside another hotel. "This isn't the one I've just left," he said. "It seemed best to find somewhere where they haven't seen us before."

The reception desk bore a small plaque that read Jenny. Jenny herself was a bored-looking young woman who came to life when she recognized Flynn. "I'd like a double room please," he told her. "My name is Smith."

"Hey," she breathed ecstatically, "Aren't you—?"

"John Smith." He gave her a knowing wink and added significantly, "Mr. and Mrs. Smith."

"Mr. and Mrs. Smith." Jenny nodded to let him know his secret was safe with her.

"Why don't you just give your real name?" Toni chuckled.

"And risk my wife finding out?" he demanded, scandalized. "Not to mention your husband. Have you forgotten what he said he'd do to me if he found me within a mile of you?"

Madness seized Toni. She gave an inane giggle and gazed up into Flynn's face with a theatrical parody of adoration. "Don't you worry," she purred. "I can handle him. Just you get me that part in the show you promised..."

Jenny's eyes were like saucers.

Flynn cleared his throat, the picture of embarrassment. "Of course I will, sweetie. But in the meantime..."

"In the meantime, I'm going to be as nice as pie to you, just as soon as we get upstairs." She continued in a provocative singsong, "I've brought that little black satin you-know-what that you like so much."

A lecherous gleam appeared in Flynn's eyes. He took the key Jenny held out to him, murmured, "I know I can rely on your discretion," and departed in the direction of the elevator, his arm firmly around Toni.

The porter accompanied them with their bags, forcing them to stand in solemn silence while the elevator rose. Toni's face ached from the effort of keeping it straight, and she didn't dare meet Flynn's eye. But stronger than laughter was the excitement rising within her as she thought of sharing passion with him again. Her heart was beating so loudly that she was sure the porter could hear.

At last they came to a halt on the second floor. They followed the porter into their room, where Flynn thrust a note into his hand and ushered him out. Before the door had closed Toni was in Flynn's arms.

In the corridor the porter looked at the size of the tip, gulped, and went down to tell Jenny she'd got it all wrong. He knew a honeymoon couple when he saw one.

Flynn and Toni were reveling in the bliss of rediscovery. No kiss had ever been so sweet, no sensations so thrilling. The lonely years apart hadn't dimmed the memory of his mouth on hers, and now she found it was as warm and ardent as she'd dreamed it to be. She returned his kiss a thousandfold, telling him with her lips and tongue what she feared to say in words.

They broke apart, but only long enough to throw aside their heavy outer clothing. Then he drew her down onto the bed and they were in each other's arms again. But he stopped what he was doing a moment to look down on her, lying there. There was hesitancy in his eyes, and she knew he was wondering if she'd freeze on him as she had the last time. "Come here," she whispered softly.

He didn't need telling twice. His mouth locked onto hers. She parted her lips and at once he slid his tongue inside, exploring the satiny flesh, teasing her with small, flickering attacks until she sighed with pleasure.

His fingers were working on the buttons of her shirt until at last he could pull it open. He released the front clasp of her bra and pulled back from her to gaze lovingly at her breasts. They were surprisingly generous next to the petiteness of the rest of her and he gave a deep sigh of satisfaction.

The reverence in his eyes brought her a surge of happiness as he caressed the rosy peaks. Her breath had caught in her throat at the feel of his fingers playing languidly with one nipple. It was already growing firm with expectancy, and his touch brought it to a hard point of passion. Then he dropped his head and let his tongue take up the work while he moved his hands down to her waist. She was hardly aware of the deft movements that opened the fastening of her jeans. The world had contracted to the sensations forking through her from the tip of his tongue as he traced a circular path again and again around the taut nipple.

She felt him slowly ease the zipper down, and then the touch of his hands on the swell of her hips. He drew back slightly to slide her jeans and panties off and toss them away. At once Toni reached up and began to pull open his buttons. She wanted to see the lean, hard body she'd loved, to feel his nakedness against hers.

He helped her by stripping off his shirt, but when she went to work on his jeans he relaxed and watched her. The deep rise and fall of his chest told her that the fever inside him was mounting as high as her own, but that he was forcing it under control, the better to enjoy the prolonged anticipation.

Her fingers were shaking so much as she undid the button that it slipped out of her grasp. She heard Flynn's soft, delighted laugh at this sign of her eagerness and glanced up to look at him. His eyes were hot with passion, and his wide, curving mouth wasn't quite steady as he felt her undress him. She returned quickly to her task, and in a moment was drawing his jeans and briefs down over his hips. What she discovered beneath thrilled her. Flynn's desire was uncompromisingly evident, and she boldly curved her hands around him, savoring his maleness.

He reached for her, pulling at her remaining garments. She tossed them aside and went back eagerly to his arms, gasping with pleasure as she felt his nakedness next to her own. She let her hands glide over his skin, enjoying him as she would have enjoyed returning to a home where she'd been happy.

Home wasn't any of the places where they'd once lived together, nor was it the little basement apartment of which she'd been so proud. Home was this beloved man, wherever he was. She'd understood that instinctively ten years ago and followed him without a backward glance. In those days her heart had had a wisdom that it later lost; but now it had all come flooding back.

With every new touch she opened familiar doors and rediscovered old delights. Here were the long thighs, lean but muscular, the narrow hips and flat stomach, the firm, masculine buttocks. Now that he was naked she could see he was a little heavier, but he'd been, if anything, too slim, and the extra bulk suited his tall frame. She'd left an attractive boy. In his place she found a man in his prime.

Flynn, too, was exploring. Her body came to new, burning life as it felt the longed-for touch of his hands roving over it, seeking out the swells and valleys of her soft flesh, lingering on the places that he'd once made his own, and which had never belonged to anyone but him. She arched herself against him, seeking his caresses in an ecstasy of sensual abandon. A low moan of desire broke from her. She wanted him so much and this waiting was torture.

But, even though his need was manifestly as urgent as her own, Flynn seemed in no hurry. He caressed her with slow, luxurious movements as though savoring a priceless treasure regained. Waves of pleasure enveloped her, until her entire body pulsated to their rhythm.

"Flynn..." she pleaded.

"I was afraid you didn't want me," he murmured.

"Oh, yes...I want you," she said raggedly. "You know I do."

He caressed the tender spot below one ear with his lips. "I'm going to make you want me more yet," he whispered. "More and then more, until there's nothing else in the world...because that's how I want you."

He lowered his head, lingeringly teasing one nipple with his lips. The sensation drove her half mad with delight and she reached for him, trying to draw him over herself and envelop him between her legs. He smiled at the eager passion in her face and let her possess him as she pleased. He slipped between her thighs, feeling her body sweetly welcome him, and in another moment they were united as though they'd never been apart.

Toni was frenzied with the longing to feel at one with him again, but the moment it happened her fever mounted still higher. The feel of him under her hands, the tangy scent of him in her nostrils: she could never have enough of these things. Her senses had starved for so long and now they were offered a banquet whose choice of riches made her dizzy.

He reclaimed her with slow, strong movements that told of the virile power of his hips and thighs. She moaned and arched against him as the heat spread out from her loins to envelop her until at last the same fire consumed them both.

Somehow she found herself lying quietly in his arms, her naked body pressed against his, all passion spent and only an infinite tenderness in its place. Flynn was so silent that she thought he'd fallen asleep, but when she looked up he was watching her broodingly. "I never forgot you, Toni," he said simply.

"I didn't forget you, either," she whispered.

Then she knew by his breathing that he really was sleeping. She snuggled against him, wondering how she could ever have been so blind as to think her love was dead. For her, there was only this man in all the world. That had been true from the first moment she'd met him, and it would be true till the end of her days.

Seven

She awoke to find Flynn looking down at her with a quizzical half smile on his face. "Hello," he said.

"Hello," she said, smiling up at him.

"I'm so glad to discover that you still do it."

She looked at him blankly. "Still do what?"

"When you were on the verge of waking up you used to give a little mutter that sounded like 'fish and chips.' You still do. I always liked that."

She began to laugh at the absurdity. Of all the things Flynn might have said to her at this moment he'd managed to find the most unexpected. How like him to take her by surprise.

He bent and kissed her and she wrapped her arms around his neck, but almost at once he shivered and drew back. "This isn't the weather for lying about like this," hc complained.

They'd slept for three hours and now it was late afternoon and the light was fading. Toni realized that there was a distinct nip in the air and shivered too. "I'm ravenous," she said. "I haven't had anything to eat since last night on the train."

"Let's go out and I'll see if I can find you a cheese sandwich," he said handsomely.

"Isn't Mr. Smith going to buy his lady friend champagne and caviar?" she teased.

"Certainly not!" he said firmly. "Mr. Smith's lady friend promised she'd brought her black satin you-know-what, and he's still waiting for a sight of it." He kissed her nose. "No goodies till you keep your side of the bargain."

Laughing like children they helped each other to dress and ran out of the hotel hand in hand. In the next street Toni stopped in front of a fish-and-chip shop and pressed her nose against the window. "I was going to buy you a huge steak," Flynn protested.

"But if we get something here," she pointed out, "we could take it back and eat it in our room."

"With you wearing your black satin you-know-what?" he inquired hopefully.

"Mr. Smith, I have a confession to make," she said meekly. "I was lying. I didn't bring my black satin you-know-what."

He struck his forehead. "Now she tells me! After I lavished fourpence on her! Is there no end to the perfidy of women?"

Two respectable matrons with shopping baskets viewed him with alarm and scuttled past hastily. Toni buried her giggles against Flynn's coat. "I'll tell you this," he said firmly, "I'm going to buy you a you-know-what, and you'll wear it, or no part in the show for you."

"Excuses, excuses!" she jeered. "You weren't going to give me a part anyway. You don't want me to meet your wife."

"That's true," he mused. "If the dragon set eyes on a sexy little number like you, she'd know I'd been up to no good."

"Well, let's get some fish and chips and hurry back, then you can get up to no good again," she murmured.

They went into the shop and selected a feast of fried cod, pickled gherkins and mountains of chips, all wrapped in newspaper. A visit to a wine shop came next and then they ran back to the hotel to lock themselves in their room, huddle under the bedclothes, and shut out the world.

They ate in bed with their fingers and drank the wine from the simple bathroom glasses. Toni, leaning blissfully against Flynn, found it hard to remember how miserable she'd been only a few hours ago. That had been another world.

"We used to eat fish and chips in bed all the time," she said. "Do you remember?"

"Mmm! That was why you talked about it in your sleep. It was all we could afford." He disposed of another gherkin. "I haven't eaten as well as this for years." He sighed.

"I thought you liked the champagne-and-oysters life."

"I do, but this is more fun." As if to prove the point he eased a hand down beneath the covers to retrieve a crumb of fish. His fingers brushed one full breast, lingering longer than was strictly necessary. "I can't seem to find it," he complained.

"You've got the wrong side," she told him severely.

"I'm sorry." He shifted his hand to explore the other breast. "Is that better?"

She drew a ragged breath. Tremors were beginning to go through her, starting from the nipple that his fingers were caressing in absentminded fashion. "It's slipped down farther," she said, looking at him innocently.

"In that case I think we'd better make a proper search." He whisked the blanket away in a moment and studied her satiny skin with deep concentration. "Not a sign," he announced.

"Nonsense, there it is." Toni retrieved the crumb but in a flash Flynn had taken it from her and swallowed it.

"Not a sign," he said firmly. "I'll just have to keep looking." His hand outlined the curves of her breasts before sliding down to her stomach and making lazy, circling movements. "Who'd ever think," he said, "that you were so nicely round under those boyish clothes? I always loved seeing you in jeans and baggy sweaters. It made me feel I knew a secret about you. Here—" he lovingly traced the indent of her tiny waist, then flared his fingers out over her hip "—and here—" his hand encompassed the roundness of her bottom. "This was all mine. That meant everything to me."

"It was always yours," she murmured huskily. Her body was caught up in the skilled enchantment he was practicing on it, and it was difficult to speak.

"And now it's mine again." He moved over her as he spoke and she moaned in sweet delight as he asserted his claim in actions as well as words.

All her senses were open to his invasion—the touch of him against her flesh, his musky, masculine scent in her nostrils. He was inside her, possessing her and possessed by her. The fire that they'd once thought dead had reignited at a touch, and it was as though time had stood still. Their perfect physical harmony was still there, telling each of them that they'd only been waiting for this moment.

He made love to her with tantalizing slowness. When she would have urged him on to the supreme moment of their union he lovingly held her back, allowing time for every movement and sensation to be savored to the last. His eyes lingered on her face, which was flushed with desire and smiling up into his with a vulnerable joy that made something catch in his throat. When she cried out for release he put all his strength and skill at her service to make the gift perfect and found that her gifts were showered on him.

Afterward he cradled her tenderly in his arms, feeling her head grow heavy on his chest. "Flynn," she murmured drowsily against his neck.

"Mmm?"

"I thought you said you only meant to be friendly?"

"Well, you can't get any friendlier than this."

Toni sighed at his evasive answer and fell asleep in his arms.

She awoke to the blissful sensation of Flynn's caresses, so that the passion of night and the passion of morning became one. He loved her into wakefulness, rousing her gently till she was ready for him, then claiming her with a vigor that drove the last of sleep away. She surveyed him with wonder, dazzled at the magic he had at his fingertips, on his lips, in his loins, and all of it for her delight.

It was nearly midday when they rose. They ravenously ate breakfast and lunch combined, then went out for a walk around the town. The Christmas lights glowed through the winter gloom, adding cheer to the otherwise dismal weather. At the corner a man stood roasting chestnuts over a brazier and they bought two packets, then wandered along munching the delicious hot treat. They stopped at the main store to stare into the window packed with toys, over which hung a sign: Santa Welcomes Children Of All Ages To His Magic Grotto. Toni and Flynn looked at each other, sharing the same thought.

"I haven't visited Father Christmas for years," she said wistfully as he took her hand and they went in.

"You've forgotten how to be a child," Flynn told her. "That's why you were never a completely successful actor."

It was true, she realized. The best actors had something of the child in them. They weren't childish, but they could be childlike when the need arose. Flynn's own contradictory nature contained some strangely opposing elements. He was as tough and cynical as a tycoon when it came to the terms of his contract, but onstage he could suspend disbelief and play "Let's pretend" with a lack of self-consciousness that gave every role total conviction. He was completely at ease now, wandering into the "grotto" and enjoying the painted scenery and colored lights as uninhibitedly as a youngster. And the force of his imagination was so powerful that Toni found herself seeing it all through his eyes.

This is what he does, she thought. This is how he gets an audience in the palm of his hand, because he can make anyone believe anything. I wish I knew what to believe.

At the center of the grotto sat Father Christmas arrayed in scarlet robes and a huge white beard. He had a child on his knee and was listening intently. "Are you going to tell him what you want?" Flynn whispered in her ear.

"What I want can't be brought down the chimney," she whispered back.

"Tell me. Perhaps I can get it for you."

It was on the tip of her tongue to blurt out that what she wanted was his love, but she stopped herself in time. She was still a long way from understanding Flynn's heart. His delightful foolery was, in its own way, a barrier.

"Is it something I can give you?" he persisted.

"Of course it is," she said lightly. "It's something *only* you can give me."

"Then it's yours, whatever it is." Flynn's voice held the faintest edge of tension. "Tell me, Toni."

The impulse to speak the truth was almost overpowering, but she only smiled and said, "You know what it is."

He smiled. "Tell me anyway. I want to hear you say it."

"I want a great big West End hit, and that's something that only my leading man can give me."

His smile faded. "Nonsense!" he said, almost angrily. "Nobody can give you that but yourself."

"In one sense, yes. But I'm a realist, and I know it isn't because of me that the advance bookings are so good. The show stands or falls by you, Flynn." To her surprise he was scowling. "Hey, don't take it so seriously. I only meant that I know who the real star is."

The scowl vanished to be replaced by a wry expression. "In that case you'd better throw a penny in Santa's magic fountain and make a wish."

Laughing, she did so, closing her eyes and wishing hard. Flynn watched her, and when she opened her eyes he said, "It's yours if I can manage it." He, too, threw a penny into the little fountain and closed his eyes for a moment.

"What was your wish?" she said when he'd finished.

"The same as yours, but I want *you* to give it to *me.* No actor can do it alone." He slipped an arm around her shoulders and said lightly, "I guess we'd better form a mutual protection society, because if ever two people needed each other it's us."

As he swept her out of the grotto she said, "I feel guilty. That's the first either of us have mentioned the show, but we should be thinking about it all the time."

"No, we shouldn't. I brought you away to forget the show. We were all getting stale. Everything will look different after a short break. Believe me, Toni, Dr. Flynn knows what he's talking about."

Before they left the store he sought out the cosmetic department and bought a bottle of the most terrifyingly expensive perfume that Toni had ever seen. "I do hope she's worth it," she said demurely.

"She is," he assured her.

On the next floor he guided her firmly into a department selling delicate lingerie and bought a minute black satin bra edged with lace, tiny panties to match, and a pair of black silk stockings. "I've never even worn stockings," she whispered. "How do they stay up?"

"You wear them with garters, preferably frilly ones—didn't your education include *anything* that mattered?"

She choked and said gravely, "I'm afraid not. They wasted my time with a lot of stuff about algebra and the source of the Nile, but nobody mentioned frilly garters. I don't suppose they sell them in this place. It looks very respectable."

"We pride ourselves on a comprehensive stock, madam," the sales assistant said reprovingly, and produced a box full of garters. Carefully avoiding Toni's eye Flynn surveyed the collection with awesome seriousness and finally chose a pair made of delicate black lace.

When they got back into the street the wind was blowing harder than ever and the pavements glistened from a recent rainfall, but Toni felt as if she were walking through fields of spring flowers.

They stocked up at a fast food bar and hurried back to the hotel. All the way there Toni was entertaining delicious fantasies of showing off her new lingerie, but when they arrived nothing seemed to go according to plan. When she started for the bathroom, declaring she wanted to shower, Flynn promptly decided that he too needed a shower and couldn't possibly wait. They soaped each other down, rinsed each other off and dried with the same huge towel, and in the inevitable confusion of limbs matters took their own course. Curled up blissfully against him afterward, Toni muttered, "Who needs special underwear, anyway?"

She awoke first and raised herself on an elbow to study him, thinking how long it had been since she'd seen Flynn sleeping and off guard. She surveyed his face with delight, discovering again how cleverly nature had constructed it. The features were unusually fine for a man—all except his nose, whose uncompromising masculinity gave weight and character to the whole construction. His lips had a slightly curved shape even in repose so that he always appeared on the edge of laughter. It was a wide mouth, which gave his smile a brilliance that seemed to reach out and touch people.

For the first time Toni noticed that there were shadows under his eyes that hadn't been there a few weeks ago, as though he, too, were reacting to the strain of an approaching opening night. She remembered how he'd always suffered from stage fright, growing tense as the date neared. But there'd been no sign of this recently, and she'd assumed he'd conquered his nerves. Now it occurred to her that he'd been hiding them for some reason. She longed to kiss the weariness away from his face, but held back in case she woke him.

Gently she pulled the sheet away so that she could study his chest. Her eyes followed it lovingly down toward his hips, and stopped there, drawn by something she hadn't noticed before. A scar ran from close to his navel toward his hipbone. He'd never mentioned an injury, and the sight of the thin white line hurt her because it was a reminder that she no longer shared his life. Tentatively she reached out a finger, then changed her mind and dropped her head to kiss it gently. At once Flynn opened his eyes. "Hey," he protested sleepily, "if you're gong to do that, I want to be awake to enjoy it."

She threw herself into his arms and kissed him vigorously till he was alert. "You never told me you'd hurt yourself," she said.

"I forgot about it. It was nothing."

"Nothing? A scar that size? What did you do?"

He shrugged. "I forget now."

She looked at him wryly. "Oh, I see."

"What does that mean?"

"I suppose that's a memento from an indignant husband. You could have told me. I don't claim possessor's rights anymore."

She turned away to slide off the bed but he held her and firmly shifted her onto her back. "When will you get it out of your head that I'm Casanova?" he demanded, holding her down.

"You were always inclined that way," she retorted, struggling to free herself, without success.

"Yes, I did a bit of flirting," he agreed. "But tell me this, Toni, did you ever find me in the wrong bed?" His eyes, holding hers, had a dangerous glint that she'd never seen before.

"All right. No," she admitted.

"Good. Just as long as we've got it straight." He released her.

"If it wasn't a husband, was it Liz Watkins?" Toni persisted, sitting up in the bed.

"Liz who?" Flynn stared blankly.

"That appalling harpy who got her claws into you just after we split up. At least, you said she was an appalling harpy; I never met her. We were all set to get a divorce and you asked me to stay married for a while to 'protect' you. Flynn, don't tell me you don't even remember."

"Oh, yes, Liz Watkins," Flynn said hastily, his brow clearing. "Of course I remember. No, it was nothing to do with Liz. We parted amicably."

"So why don't you want to tell me how you got the scar?" she demanded.

"What does it matter how I got the damned scar?"

"It wouldn't if you weren't making a secret of it."

He scowled. "If you must know, I fell off an elephant."

"You *what*?"

"I said I fell off an elephant. Toni, if you dare laugh—"

But she was laughing already, leaning against him and rocking with mirth. He joined in reluctantly. "It was when I was making a film in India. I had to sit on this elephant in full brigand costume. Nobody warned me it was a circus elephant. The minute someone blew a horn it did a handstand and I went straight over its head. And don't you ever dare repeat this story. It wouldn't do my image any good."

When she'd recovered her composure Toni asked, "But that still doesn't explain how you got the scar."

"I had a knife tucked in my belt."

"And you fell on it? Good grief, you could have been killed."

"Well, I wasn't. It was only a scratch, much to the relief of the producer."

"To hell with the producer!" she said. She looked at him sadly, realizing how little she knew of his life during the past four and a half years. "I wish you'd told me. After all," she added with a little laugh, "we're supposed to be friends, and friends should share things."

"It happened fairly soon after you left me. You weren't in a very friendly mood. Neither was I, if it comes to that. I felt you'd deserted me when I needed you, and I was bitter."

"But you never needed me," she said, her eyes wide. "You were so self-sufficient...all of you. You could be so many people I never knew who I was living with from one day to the next."

He shrugged. "I believe in varying the company," he said lightly. "None of me hung around long enough to bore you, did they?"

"You couldn't bore me, Flynn. But you didn't have to entertain me all the time. I married one man and I found myself living with hundreds."

He was watching her intently, "But you always knew it was me underneath."

"Did I? I'm not sure. Where was 'underneath'? Every time you removed one mask and I'd look for the real man, I'd see another mask. Even when you seemed most yourself I used to wonder if you were playing a part called 'the real Flynn Rawley.'" She stopped, for his face had paled and taken on a bleak look. "I'm sorry," she said hastily. "I didn't mean to be unkind. It's in the past now. I expect I've gotten it all wrong."

"No, you haven't," he said, speaking lightly but with an obvious effort. "It's just that...oh hell, as you say, it's all in the past. We're having a wonderful time. Let's not spoil it by dragging up old ghosts."

Now, she thought, she knew where she stood. He didn't see this as the prelude to reviving their marriage; it was simply part of "Dr." Flynn's cure for the blues. They were just two good friends, clinging to each other for support in a nerve-racking situation. The past was shut away, beyond recall or repair, and his suddenly tense manner when she tried to talk about it told its own story.

"How about eating that food we bought?" she said, smiling at him.

"Great idea!" he said, with obvious relief that she'd dropped the subject.

While they ate Flynn pulled out a newspaper he'd bought in the street. By chance it fell open at a full-page advertisement.

"Opening Soon," the headline read, "Flynn Rawley in *The Merry War.*"

"See what I mean about who's the real star?" Toni said. "There's your name above the title and there's mine—" she ran her eyes down the page "—well, it must be somewhere." She became aware that Flynn hadn't responded to her clowning. Looking up she saw the same strained look on his face that she'd noticed as he slept. "You still get stage fright?" she asked gently.

"If anything it's worse," he confessed. "Climbing the ladder's fun, but balancing on top when you get there is hell. You'll find that out."

"If I ever get there."

"You'll be up there after opening night," he assured her.

"Flynn, do you really think so?" she pleaded. "Because sometimes I get the willies thinking of your reputation in my hands."

"That's strange," he said with a wan smile, "because I get the willies thinking that this is your big chance, and I might be the one to spoil it for you. It's so terribly important . . ."

"It's nice of you to feel for me," she said warmly, "but you mustn't worry. If I fail, it'll be my fault, not yours. Besides—'' she shrugged and tried to sound casual ''—there's always another chance.''

''No,'' Flynn said slowly. ''There'll never be another chance.''

Toni stared at him, puzzled. Flynn had spoken more to himself than to her, and he was looking past her at something she couldn't see.

''You have to know the vital moment when it comes, and seize it,'' he continued in the same distracted tone, ''because if you let it slip through your fingers . . . you can waste the rest of your life in useless regrets.''

''Flynn . . .''

He seemed to become aware of her. ''So we won't let that happen,'' he said firmly. ''We'll make this the big one for both of us.'' His voice was cheerful again, and Toni had a strange feeling, as though a mask had slipped momentarily and been hastily adjusted.

Eight

Flynn picked up the paper again and became absorbed in the sports results. It was clear he didn't want to talk anymore. Toni watched him for a moment, then rested her chin on her hand and became sunk in thought. After a while her eyes lit up and she gave a little smile that Flynn didn't see. She began to clear away the remains of their meal, tossing everything into the waste bin and brushing crumbs from the bed, her brow furrowed with true housewifely fervor.

"Couldn't this wait?" Flynn asked plaintively. "You're bouncing me up and down and I can't read the print."

"Sorry," she said with dreadful heartiness. "It's just that I don't like to see a mess. Besides, I want this all out of the way so that I can have an early night. You wouldn't believe how worn out I am, and my back..." She clasped the small of her back and made a face.

"I'm sorry. Can I do anything, give you a massage?"

"Later, perhaps. I've got some stuff to rub into it. It smells rather nasty, but you won't mind that, will you?"

"Of course not," he said bravely.

"I may need a hot-water bottle as well." She began to rummage in her luggage until she found a jar of face cream and a bag of hair curlers, both of which she pushed into the plastic shopping bag they'd acquired in the store that afternoon. Out of the corner of her eye she saw Flynn's fascinated horror as he observed this performance, and she suppressed a chuckle. She completed the picture by taking up her modest nightgown and pushing it into the bag too. "I'll have a nice hot shower and then get ready for bed," she told him. At the door of the bathroom she paused and asked in a weary voice, "Do you think if you called room service they'd send me up some cocoa?"

"Cocoa?" he said faintly.

"Well, anyway, it can wait until later." She savored a last look at his glum face, then escaped into the bathroom before her mirth overcame her. That should give him something to worry about, she reckoned.

After a shower she took up the bag, pulled out the face cream, curlers and nightie and dumped them all in a corner. At the bottom of the bag were the parcels Flynn had bought in the perfume and lingerie departments. Hurriedly Toni set to work, and a few minutes later she was able to survey herself with satisfaction.

She didn't recognize the seductive creature who looked back at her from the mirror, but these past few days had taught her that to be someone else was a way of revealing yourself. Flynn's creation of "Mr. and

Mrs. Smith'' had freed both of them from the constraints of their real situation, allowing them to communicate in a new way. As a teenager Toni had been overawed by Flynn's apparent mastery of life, his easy success, his ability to make magic happen. Even now, she hadn't quite shaken off the lack of confidence that had always plagued her where he was concerned.

But ''Mrs. Smith'' was a woman who knew her own erotic powers and was sublimely confident of the spell she could cast over ''Mr. Smith.'' That deceptively petite body contained a subtle sensuality that he couldn't resist because it harmonized so perfectly with his own. Giving ''Mrs. Smith'' one last approving look in the mirror, Toni opened the bathroom door and stood looking at Flynn, sunk in the sports pages. She waited a moment, one hand resting on the doorpost, one hip thrust slightly forward to emphasize its beautiful curve. ''Good evening, Mr. Smith,'' she said softly.

He glanced up with half his attention, and immediately did a violent double take that thrilled her completely. He stayed quite still, as if totally stunned, but gradually the astonishment on his face gave way to admiration and relish. ''Good evening,'' he said politely. ''Is it Mrs. Smith or—no—'' Studying her face he detected something new and pleasurably unexpected. ''I don't think I've ever met *you* before,'' he said slowly and with a questioning look.

She swayed toward him, noting with delight that he seemed to be having some difficulty in breathing. His eyes followed the lines of her breasts, which were barely encompassed by the wispy black bra, then down to her tiny waist and on again to trace the swell of her hips and the delicate lines of the black satin panties. Last of all he took in the slender, elegant lines of her legs, sheathed in black silk stockings supported by a pair of extremely provocative garters.

"That's right," she assured him. "We've never met before." She raised one silk-clad leg and placed the toe on the bed near to him, looking down with an enticing half smile. Almost hypnotized, he reached out to caress her slender ankle, then slowly traced the lovely line of her calf. His eyes never left her face.

His fingers trembled as they lingered on her slim thigh, but when he tried to explore further she laughed and twisted tantalizingly away from him. She came to rest on the end of the bed, her eyes mocking him as she removed the garter and tossed it away. Then she lazily swung her leg around until it pointed to him, placed her toes against his chest and flexed them gently.

Flynn drew in a ragged breath as the sensations aroused by those teasing movements went through him. "No," he said with meaning, "we've *never* met before. But we should have. If I'd know you were around..." He was working as he spoke, drawing the stocking smoothly down her leg until it was off.

"But I wasn't," she said softly. "I was never around before this. After all, people come and go; you should know that better than anyone."

He grinned at this reference to his own multitude of personalities. "Taking a leaf from my book, huh?" he growled. He made a lunge for her but she was too quick for him. She writhed away, leaping up from the bed to stand looking down at him.

"Let's say I'm making a small experiment," she teased. "The results might be interesting. You never know."

He succeeded in catching hold of her wrist and drawing her close enough to wrap his arm around her waist. Then he released her hand and enfolded her with his other arm. He held her like that, imprisoned in his embrace, his face pressed against the smooth skin just below her breasts. Toni twined her fingers in his hair, drawing him closer still, feeling his breath burn her.

With a swift movement Flynn drew back, pulling her down onto the bed with him, still his prisoner. "That perfume is wicked," he murmured. "Don't ever wear it near any other man. You wouldn't be safe."

"I don't feel very safe now," she whispered. "But then, who wants to be safe?" She seemed to become aware of his fingers working at the other stocking, and said with an air of innocent surprise, "I only put these clothes on five minutes ago."

"Don't worry, they've done their work," he assured her fervently. "They were meant for removing, not wearing." He was taking his own words to heart, easing the stocking down her leg with slow, sensual appreciation. "Mrs. Smith," he murmured, "you're sensational."

Toni's heart was pounding as the tide of hot magic rose and threatened to engulf her. It was an effort to keep him at a distance and tempt him little by little, when what she wanted to do was throw herself into his arms and tell him that she was all his. But she made herself hold back, knowing that Flynn was finding a new kind of enchantment in her witchery.

He was working feverishly with the clasp of the bra, pulling it away from her to gaze down on her breasts with eyes filled with wonder, as though he was seeing them for the first time. Yet even now there was a gleam of humor in his eyes. "You little minx," he whispered. "Frightening me with all that talk about cocoa and hot-water bottles."

"Serves you right for being so easily fooled," she said, teasing him. "As though I would—"

The last word was cut off as he smothered her mouth with his own. His arms were around her, thrilling her with their strength, while he moved his lips insistently against hers, urging her to yield. She did so, sighing with pleasure as his tongue found its way inside, exploring the moist warmth.

He had begun to rove over the curves and valleys of her body with his free hand, and the light touch of his fingers trailing across her stomach set off sensations that flowed through her in ripples. Her toes curled in anticipation and she brushed them against his leg, letting him know, wordlessly, what his skilled lovemaking was doing to her.

He'd reached the swell of her breast and was exploring it in a leisurely fashion, taking his time to reach the top where the nipple was already hardening in expectation. He caressed it tenderly, relishing the feeling of making this woman flower for him.

He released her mouth. His breath was coming raggedly and his eyes, as they swept over her, were hot with anticipation. She met his gaze with one of her own in which surrender and conquest were mixed equally.

He dropped his head to her breast and teased the nipple with his lips to a peak of desire, making tremors of pleasure go through her. She abandoned herself to that sensual ecstasy, closing her eyes and arching her body against him in a silent affirmation of her mounting passion.

Shudders possessed her as she felt his lips on her other breast. She reached out, entwined her hands in his hair, then ran them over his shoulders, feeling the ripple of muscles beneath the skin.

He slid his fingers down until they reached the tiny panties and were inching their way under, but Toni wriggled away suddenly out of his grasp.

"Hey..." he protested.

"Let's not rush things, Mr. Smith," she purred, pushing him onto his back and beginning to flex her fingers against his chest. "I haven't even started yet."

His eyes were alight with appreciation, but he said huskily, "I'm all for getting every last second out of this, but I don't know how long I have."

She followed his gaze downward to where the urgency of his desire was plainly told and smiled in deep feminine satisfaction. He saw it and growled, "Pleased with yourself, aren't you?"

She was lying beside him, propped up on one elbow, her free hand tracing languid circles around his navel. "It's you I'm trying to please," she said. "Of course, if I'm not succeeding...?" She widened the movements of her fingers, tracing feather-light patterns over a wider area and felt him tremble.

"You're succeeding," he said thickly. He lay back and surrendered himself to her magic as her fingertips softly provoked him in a thousand ways. When he could stand it no longer he seized her hand and drew the palm to his mouth where his tongue conducted a series of flickering attacks that made her breath come harder.

He drew her forward by her shoulders until she lay on top of him, and wrapped the other arm about her, making her his prisoner. Lying blissfully against his chest Toni felt his fingers trace patterns on her spine until both hands joined over her hips and slid beneath the elastic of her panties to encompass her bottom. "This time they're coming off," he said firmly.

"Unless you've got six-foot arms you'll never get them down to my feet," she pointed out.

A sudden tension in his shoulders and the sound of ripping fabric told her how he'd disposed of the problem. Then he rolled over, pinning her neatly, and her legs parted willingly for him, inviting his entry. She was aching to feel him inside her, and now that ache was satisfied. The moment of their union was like the first time ever, dizzying, blissful, a moment outside of time and space.

Despite the long, tantalizing game she'd played with him Flynn was still sufficiently in command not to hurry. He made love with slow, easy movements that heightened her desire while they tortured her with the promise of contentment to come. With every deep thrust she moaned softly in a wordless plea for release, but the promise was still unfulfilled while her craving mounted.

She could feel the tensing and flexing of the steel muscles of his back as he claimed and reclaimed her, moving more quickly as the moment of truth drew near. Toni abandoned herself totally to the thrilling sensations that only he could bring her. The mask of the siren had fallen from her now, and there remained only the woman in love—if he had eyes to see her and a heart to understand. She arched against him, whispering his name repeatedly as every movement brought her closer to the final ecstasy. It came at last, a joy that swept over her senses, annihilating her and bringing her to new life in the same moment. Her voice became a cry, pleading for it never to be over, even while she knew that it was already and they were separate again.

Half of herself seemed to have been torn away as he left her, and the other half would be lonely and desolate till it was made whole with him again.

Flynn lay awake for a long time that night, watching over her. He saw with pleasure that some of the weariness and desperation had gone from her face. He wished they could have had longer, but tomorrow they'd have to drive back to London.

He'd done his best for her, but now he wondered if it had been the right "best." How could he know what she needed? Once, he'd thought he understood her completely. His lips curled in self-mockery as he remembered how that piece of arrogance had been knocked out of him: she'd left him, proving that he'd known nothing about her at all.

There were a million things he'd have liked to tell her over the past two days, but he'd forced himself to stay silent, refusing to add to her burdens. The old specter of stage fright that had always haunted him was twice as grim this time, because he carried her dreams on his shoulders. But he'd denied the fear and presented a laughing face to her. He'd encouraged her to lean on him, but he hadn't leaned on her, although the temptation to do so had been great.

Perhaps he'd have yielded to that temptation but for a memory that tormented him. The face of Alec Wrighton would rise in his mind, and he'd hear again that self-satisfied voice saying, "You gave me the impression you never had been very much in love...an adolescent infatuation that you'd outgrown." And Toni's face, suddenly alert, as though she'd heard a truth that she'd never fully understood before.

He wondered what had been in her mind while she'd laughed and loved with him these past two days. She'd once likened the early days of their marriage to the heedless play of children, and he'd encouraged her to become a child again, leaving the cares to him, with nothing to do but enjoy herself. Now he wondered if he'd freed her from care only to send her back into the arms of Alec Wrighton.

With a swift movement he cradled her in his arms, holding her close to his heart. If he achieved nothing else he'd save her from that.

Toni felt the movement and the sweet sensation of being enfolded in warmth. The throb of his heart against hers seemed to pulse through her flesh. She stirred and curved her arms up around his neck, but she didn't awaken.

Nine

Late on Sunday evening Flynn drew his car up outside Toni's front door. "Here we are," he said. "I've gotten you home safe and sound."

"Come inside and I'll make you something."

"Thanks, but no. I'm worn out after that drive. I'll go straight home and flake out."

"Why bother? You can stay here."

She tried to keep a plea out of her voice and just stopped herself adding "Stay as long as you like." The next moment she was glad she'd bitten the words back because Flynn shook his head. "No, I'll be off and leave you in peace." He yawned and said sleepily, "Why do vacations ever have to end? Back to the grindstone tomorrow. Good night, Toni."

He flung an arm around her shoulders, drew her closer, and bestowed a brotherly kiss on her cheek.

Then she was out of the car and he was roaring away into the darkness.

The apartment seemed unbearably bleak and cold after being in the glow of his presence, and Toni felt as though there were a lead weight in her chest. Flynn didn't want her back. He'd been a kind, loving friend, pulling her out of the doldrums, but that was all.

She wondered if he'd realized that by making love, they'd legally revived their marriage. But he plainly hadn't. He'd made jokes about fighting the divorce, but she'd never taken those seriously, and he'd been silent on the subject recently. If he planned to hold on to her he'd surely have seized the chance he had now. Instead, he seemed oblivious, and Toni was determined to say nothing. He'd showered her with gifts of passion and laughter, for which she'd be grateful all her days, and she was too proud to repay his generosity by trying to trap him.

When rehearsals started again on Monday, everyone seemed to have benefited from time off. The bogged-down feeling vanished as the cast attacked their roles with renewed vigor, and Toni silently blessed Flynn for suggesting the break.

The day came when they were ready for the first run-through, with sets, costumes and full orchestra. Shep Dunway came to watch, and when it was over he congratulated Toni. "There are still some rough edges, of course," he said, "but it's all there. I knew I wasn't wrong about you, Toni. At this rate your next stop will be Broadway."

"Some chance," she said, laughing to hide the excited leap of her heart.

"There's more chance than you think. Greg Benskin will be in London then and I'm bringing him to the opening night."

Toni gasped. Benskin Productions was a name to conjure with on Broadway. If Greg Benskin liked her work the sky was the limit.

"He has to return to New York first thing the next morning," Shep added, "so it's lucky we don't open a day later, or we'd miss him."

She ran to tell Flynn, who hugged her and said, "How about a champagne celebration tonight?"

"I can't. I'm having dinner with Alec. He called me yesterday for the first time since he stormed out of the restaurant."

"Is he still mad at you?"

"It's much worse than that," she said miserably. "He's forgiven me."

She'd known that she couldn't marry Alec almost as soon as she'd accepted him. When they'd first met she'd seen only what she wanted to see, his quiet manner, his solidity, his quality of always being the same, which she'd wrongly equated with reliability. Because he was a contrast to Flynn she'd convinced herself that Alec was what she'd wanted. Looking back now she could see that her uneasiness about him had dated from Flynn's return.

She'd accepted Alec's proposal that night in the restaurant only because Flynn's antics had exasperated her, making Alec briefly look good again. Now she must find a kind way to say she couldn't marry him.

The dinner was as bad as she'd feared. Alec was at his most charitable, assuring her kindly that he no longer bore her any grudge for what had happened. "It wasn't your fault, darling," he said. "I should have realized that instead of flying off the handle. The person to blame is that husband of yours. You haven't been the same person since you've been working with him."

"No, that's true," she said wryly. "But it's not fair to blame him, Alec..."

"My dear, it's very sweet and loyal of you to defend him. But if you could stand back and see yourself objectively, as I can, you'd understand the disastrous effect he has on you. At one time you'd have shown far more sense of responsibility than you did that night; I'm afraid he brings out the worst in you."

"How strange you should say that," she murmured, remembering that Flynn had said the same words about Alec. She looked at him curiously. "Can you really see me objectively, Alec?"

"I hope so."

"But I thought you said you were in love with me."

"So I am, my dear, but I trust I haven't allowed it to destroy my sense of proportion."

Toni smiled and spoke almost to herself. "If you really love someone you don't have any sense of proportion about them. They're just more important than anything else in the world, and all the silly little things they do are precious, or at least forgivable because it's them."

"It's nice of you to say so, my dear." Toni gave him a startled glance, but he continued, "I can't tell you how I'm looking forward to all this being over and you being your real self again. Have you any idea when you can get a divorce?"

"Alec, I don't really think you'd enjoy being married to me. I'm afraid that what you've seen recently *is* my real self."

"Nonsense, I refuse to believe that. You've just been under a lot of strain. When we're married you won't have to endure this kind of struggle."

"But I enjoy the strain of it. You have to struggle if you're going to create something, and all the insecurity doesn't matter if the right person's there, sharing it with you. But it has to be the *right* person, someone who understands and is there for you to hold on to. That's the only security that matters."

"Is that the voice of Flynn Rawley talking?"

"Let's just say it's what he's taught me. You said yourself that he and I are birds of a feather, and it's true, although I hadn't seen it then. I'm sorry, Alec. I can't marry you."

They parted on good terms, and Toni was sure she detected the faintest hint of relief in Alec's manner.

The next morning Flynn cocked a questioning eyebrow at her calm expression. "I've told Alec I'm not going to marry him," she said.

"Good for you," Flynn said cheerfully. "I knew when it came down to it you'd have too much sense of self-preservation. Fine, I'm glad we've got that out of the way. Now there's something important I want to ask you."

"Yes?" She couldn't disguise the eagerness in her voice.

Flynn pulled out his script. "Just here," he said, riffling over the pages till he came to a scene. "I can't understand this. The first time Benedick tells Beatrice outright that he loves her, why does he say that it's strange?"

Toni was silent a moment to blunt the sharp edge of disappointment. "It seems to me," she said at last, hesitantly, "that there's love and Love. At first everything seems easy and lighthearted, but then you see the other person unhappy, and needing you. That's when superficial love fades and real love starts to hurt. Benedick's always seen Beatrice laughing, but now she's wretched and he realizes he'll do anything to comfort her—even challenge his best friend to a duel and perhaps kill him."

Flynn frowned. "But he already knew he loved her."

"Yes, but he didn't understand what it really means to love someone," she said softly, "how that person becomes the most important thing in the world. When he faces that, he understands how deep he's getting in, but this time he's not afraid. He's strong enough to make sacrifices for his love and a bit surprised to find himself so strong."

Flynn thought for a moment. "Through loving her," he said slowly, "he discovers a new depth and maturity in himself. And so he says, 'I do love nothing in the world so well as you, is not that strange?' " Flynn's voice was full of ecstatic discovery and Toni nodded, delighted at his quick understanding. "Nothing in the world," he repeated as if in a dream. "That's the answer. It explains everything. He can face the hurt of loving because nothing else in the world is so important. And when he knows that, he becomes a man. It's so simple, really, isn't it? Strange that something that simple should be so difficult." He seemed to come out of his reverie. "Thank you, Toni," he said. "You've given me the key I've been looking for all this time."

Watching him that afternoon Toni knew Flynn had found the vital "something" that added the last touch to his performance, and the sweetest thing of all was his acknowledgement that he owed it to her.

With a week to go to the opening the air was sparkling with expectancy. Toni held her breath, hardly daring to believe that everything was going so well. Like almost all theater people she was superstitious, and now she began going through small rituals. She threw salt over her shoulder, picked up nails, avoided ladders—all to placate the jealous gods who would punish her if she dared be complacent.

But when the blow fell it came from a totally unexpected direction and landed with tragic force.

One afternoon Flynn was called away to the telephone. Out of the corner of her eye Toni saw him return, and she knew at once that something had gone wrong. She called a break and took him aside. "Flynn, what's happened?"

His face was pale. "It's my mother," he said. "She's dying."

"Darling, I'm sorry." She pulled him into her arms to comfort him.

She'd met Flynn's widowed mother only twice. Mrs. Rawley had chosen to stay in Hamlaire, the small Irish town where she'd always lived. Toni had found her polite but curiously remote. She loved her son, but seemed to take little pride in his achievements. She'd made no attempt to come to London for the opening night of *The Merry War*, although he'd invited her to stay with him for as long as she liked.

"She's had a heart attack," he said. "They say she's not going to live." His eyes were on her, full of a plea for her understanding. "Toni, I must go."

"Of course you must," she said at once.

"I've got to talk to her," he said bleakly. "She *must* tell me. . ." He passed a hand over his eyes.

She wanted to ask him what he meant, but this was no time for questions. She left him a moment to speak to her secretary. "Sally's calling the airport," she said when she came back. "I've told her to book two seats on the first flight."

"Two?"

"I'm coming with you."

For a moment Flynn's face lit up, but at once he said, "Shouldn't the director stay at her post?"

"I've got an excellent assistant and he can take over for a few days," she said firmly. "I'm coming to keep a protective eye on my leading man."

Flynn was silent but the pressure of his hand on hers told her everything about his feelings. She knew he wasn't fooled by her apparent reason.

Sally came back to say she'd booked two seats on a flight that evening, the earliest she could get.

"Go home and get some things together," Toni said. "I'll come over to get you as soon as I'm packed."

She spent half an hour with George Alladale, giving him instructions for rehearsing those parts of the show that didn't involve Flynn. "How long will you both be away?" he asked.

"I don't know. As long as it takes."

"Damn! Just when things were going so well! Even when he gets back we'll have lost momentum."

"It's not Flynn's fault," Toni said sharply.

"Calm down, I realize that. It's just we all want this thing to succeed, and you've got as much riding on it as anyone."

"I suppose so," she said vaguely. It was difficult to remember how large the show had once loomed now that her mind was filled with Flynn's tragic face and the strange desperation in his voice as he'd said, "She *must* tell me . . ." There was something here that she didn't understand, but she knew her husband needed her as he never had before.

Once home, she hurriedly packed a bag and took a taxi to Flynn's luxurious apartment near the center of town. He was watching from the window for her, and when she got out of the elevator his front door was open and he was standing there. She closed the door behind them and enfolded him in her arms. Flynn held her tight, as if she were the only safety on earth.

"Is there any more news?" she asked.

"Yes, I've just called. She's still alive, but they say I should get there as soon as possible."

"Will we get a taxi that time of night? There are no trains to Hamlaire."

"I've always found a taxi before," he said vaguely. She stared at him. This wasn't like Flynn, who'd always been a practical man, often leaving her nothing to do.

"Let's not take chances." Toni picked up the phone, called Sally and reeled off briskly, "Sal, I'm at Flynn's. I want you to call Cork Airport, get the name of the best taxi company, then call them and have someone waiting for us. Give them the flight number, tell them the name is Locksley, as you did with the tickets. With any luck that'll stop the press getting wind of it for a while. Call me back at this number as soon as you have details." She hung up and turned to find Flynn staring at her as if he'd never seen her before. "Did I take too much on myself?" she asked anxiously.

"No, I'm glad you're giving the orders. I don't seem able to concentrate on practical details. It's just that I've never heard you sound so much in command before, not even at rehearsals." His voice suddenly became husky. "Thank you for coming, Toni."

She kissed him gently. "Are there any more practical details for me to see to?"

"I'd started my packing..." he said hesitantly.

A half-packed suitcase lay open on his bed. A glance inside it showed Toni that Flynn wasn't doing a very good job. "Why don't you make some coffee while I finish this?" she said. "We needn't leave for an hour."

While she packed she puzzled over why Flynn seemed to be coming apart inside. Toni knew he loved his mother, but something told her there was more to it than that. His self-sufficiency had always helped him cope with disaster, both practically and emotionally. Now he was like a man who'd been poleaxed.

On his bedside table Flynn kept a couple of photographs. One was of Toni, the other showed Flynn and his mother together. She studied it, noticing the wonderful expressive eyes they shared and the mobile mouths that were so alike.

Flynn brought the coffee from the kitchen and they sat drinking it. She longed to put her arms around him again, but instinct warned her not to. His eyes held a remote, introspective look that told her he was reliving scenes in which she had no part. Once or twice he looked up and gave her a brief smile, but immediately he returned to his sad thoughts.

She ached at being shut out, just when they seemed to be so close, and longed to plead with him to talk to her. But she stayed silent, knowing that Flynn must turn to her of his own free will, or not at all.

Sally called back to say everything was arranged, and soon they were on their way to the airport. At eleven o'clock that night they landed at Cork to find a cabdriver waiting for them. An hour's drive in darkness and slashing rain brought them to Hamlaire's tiny, cottage hospital.

The doctor appeared immediately and said, "Mrs. Rawley is holding her own for the moment, but I'm glad you got here."

Toni followed Flynn into the room where Sarah Rawley lay, attached to machines. The little woman looked much older than her fifty-five years. Her hair was short and iron gray, framing a thin face that Toni remembered as always looking weary. She was lying quite still now, breathing shallowly. Flynn approached the bed and took his mother's hand gently in his. Toni stayed back and found a chair by the wall.

Flynn hardly moved as the night wore on and the sky outside lightened slightly. His eyes were fixed on his mother's face with painful intensity, and whenever she stirred his eagerness was evident in the lines of his body. After what seemed like an age she opened her eyes, and her faint smile showed that she recognized him. Flynn leaned forward and kissed her. At once her eyes closed again.

The doctor arrived to look at Sarah, and grunted approval. "Her condition is far less precarious than I'd feared," he said.

"You mean she'll live?" Flynn asked eagerly.

"It's too soon to say. I hadn't expected her to hang on until this morning, but she has, and every hour means a better chance. There's a little café right next door. Why don't you two go and get some breakfast? I'll send for you if need be."

Flynn was on edge in the café, anxious to get back to his mother. Anxiety and sleeplessness had left his face drawn and pale. "She'll recover, I'm sure of it," Toni said. "You heard what that doctor said. She's already better."

"I wish to God I could be sure," he said tiredly. "If she does get over it I'm going to try again to persuade her to come and live in London. She's always refused before because she said she wanted to stay where she felt at home, but I must have her near me. She must come," he finished with a sudden, unexpected edge to his voice. Toni looked at him, puzzled, remembering how he'd said, "She must tell me," in that same voice. What was the mystery that Flynn couldn't share with her?

"Shall I see about finding us a hotel?" she asked.

"We might as well stay in her house. It's not far, and I have a key. Here—" he took his keys out and extracted one "—why don't you go and get settled in while I go back to the hospital? I'll call you."

It sounded reasonable enough, if only she could rid herself of the feeling that he no longer wanted her with him. She smiled to hide the aching sadness that swept her and pocketed the key. When they finished breakfast Flynn returned to the hospital while she took their bags to the little house.

The freezing wind hit her as soon as she stepped into the street. Hamlaire stood right on the southern coast of Ireland, exposed to the gales of the Atlantic. Sarah Rawley's little house was on the edge of town, the rear windows looking straight over the ocean, which was slate gray and heaving on this winter morning.

Toni found the house looking almost exactly as it had on her last visit five years ago. Sarah never changed anything if she could help it. The framed photograph of her husband, Matthew, still dominated the front room, and Toni studied it, trying to discover some resemblance to Flynn, but could see none.

Flynn called later to say that Sarah was holding her own, and he was coming home for a few hours. Her heart ached for him when he appeared, looking more strained than before. He ate the lunch she made him, but she knew he wasn't aware of what he was doing.

"You should try to get some rest," she urged when he'd finished. "You haven't slept for twenty-four hours. I'll wake you at once if there's a call."

"All right, I'll try," he said briefly, and went into the bedroom shutting the door. Toni heard him walking about for some time. She went into the kitchen to wash up, and when she came back she found Flynn in the front room. He was sitting by the fire, his eyes fixed somberly on the picture of his father. He looked up when she came in and held out a hand. "I'm giving you a hard time," he said. "I'm sorry."

She kissed him. "Don't be. I can take it. I only wish I felt I was helping you."

"You're helping me in ways you don't dream of. Just be here, Toni. I need something to hold on to, something real and solid." He looked around the room. "Something that isn't just a mask," he added softly.

Puzzled, Toni followed his gaze. To her the little room seemed totally solid, but such was Flynn's mesmeric power that for a moment she almost believed that the walls and furniture were about to dissolve into a dream. "I don't understand," she said. "This is such a down-to-earth sort of place. The first time I saw it I wondered if you became an actor as a kind of reaction against it."

"That's true, but not in the way you mean. I started acting long before I went into the theater. I began when

I was a child, because I was trying to *find* reality, not *escape* it.

She felt a sudden sharp moment of illumination. "Flynn," she said urgently, "what is it that you want your mother to tell you?"

The hand holding hers tightened suddenly and she could feel him trembling. "I want her to tell me who I really am," he said simply.

"But aren't you Sarah and Matthew Rawley's son?"

"I'm Sarah's son, but I don't think Matthew Rawley ever existed." He pointed at the picture. "That could be anyone. I'm fairly sure it wasn't my mother's husband. I don't think she ever had a husband."

"You mean you're illegitimate?"

"I'm almost sure I am."

"But surely she'd have told you by now?"

"I don't think so. Even today people are old-fashioned in this part of the world, and I was born thirty-two years ago. To have a child out of wedlock was a great scandal.

"There's always been a mysterious gap in my life where a family should have been. The Irish are friendly people with a strong family sense, but I seemed to have no relatives at all. My mother arrived in Hamlaire as a widow, just before I was born, and no one ever came visiting."

"But surely nobody'd care now?"

"I wouldn't care twopence if I knew the truth for sure. It's *not knowing* that I can't endure." His voice was ragged with pain. "If she dies without telling me the truth I don't know what I'll do."

"But perhaps she has told you the truth? Maybe you aren't illegitimate."

"I can't believe that. There are too many things not explained. Her maiden name was Connell. I've checked the public records in England and Ireland. There's no record of a marriage between Matthew Rawley and Sarah Connell in the whole twenty years before I was born, nor is there a death certificate for a Matthew Rawley just before my birth. I think when she knew she was pregnant she went away to where she wasn't known and could pass as a widow. She created a whole invented background, even to the photograph that's supposed to be of my father."

"But couldn't that actually be your father, even if they weren't married?"

"It could be, but it's a posed portrait, not a casual snapshot. If they were just ships that passed in the night I don't think she'd have a formal picture of him. Besides, look at it. What could I have in common with him?"

Toni studied the heavy, prosaic face in the picture. Sons didn't always resemble their fathers, but she felt his instinct was right about this. That earthbound man could never have fathered Flynn's mercurial genius.

"I think she probably bought it in a junk shop," he added. "It was the final touch to the illusion she was determined to create.

"She did it very well. She has a lot of imagination, and she built up a whole background, densely packed with details. But she used to slip up occasionally and contradict herself, and I started to suspect."

"But even if she admits it, suppose she only knew your father briefly? If she can't tell you anything about him, aren't you as badly off as before?"

"No, because it would be the truth. I could cope with the truth, whatever it is. What I find hard is this pretense that I'm the son of a man who never existed. It's always made me feel as though *I* didn't exist."

Flynn was silent for a long time and she could feel his tension as he forced himself to confront things he'd hidden away for years. "That's very frightening," he said at last. "It used to scare me when I was an adolescent and it still does. Sometimes I've looked down at myself and half expected to see nothing there. There's been a vacuum that I've had to fill up somehow. It was like living on a stage. My 'father's' picture was no more than a prop. My mother and I were both playing parts, but I didn't know what mine was.

"I started imagining what my father might have been—a tycoon, a burglar. Then I saw myself being those things." Flynn's face grew animated as he became again the little boy frantically searching for his own identity. "My favorite role was a master criminal. I went around for days looking furtively over my shoulder in case the police had realized that I was the mad genius behind the disappearance of the crown jewels.

"Once I decided my father had been a star acrobat in a circus. After that, whenever I vaulted over the wooden horse in the gym I ended with a flourish to acknowledge the crowd's cheers. The teachers got fed up with me, but the other kids loved it, so I started playing up to them. I had a new personality for every situation. It solved a lot of my childhood problems. I never had to confront anything because I could always get 'somebody else' to do it for me." He looked at Toni. "It wasn't till years later I realized what a dangerous thing I was doing," he said.

She put her arms around him, holding him close. Here was the explanation of Flynn's very nature, the secret that haunted the man and gave the actor his brilliance.

If only I'd known years ago, she thought. I could have understood.

"Did you ever ask her about it?"

"Yes, but she wouldn't tell me anything. If I persisted she became so upset that I had to give up. That hurt because she and I were very close in other ways. I hated the thought that she was keeping a secret from me. I thought if I waited patiently she'd tell me one day; but perhaps I've waited too long."

He leaned against her and she tightened her protective embrace, inwardly raging at her own helplessness. She'd have given anything in the world to banish that look of desperate grief from his face, but it wasn't in her power. She could only be here as long as he needed her, offering him her comfort and hoping he could take it.

The shrill cry of the telephone made them jump. Toni took one look at Flynn's face, full of dread, and reached out a hand for the receiver. When she put it down she said, "They want us to get over to the hospital. She's had another heart attack."

They found Sarah alive but there was a dark look around her eyes that told Toni what was coming. As Flynn sat by the bed she stood behind him, praying with all her heart that Sarah would find some words of comfort for her son before it was too late.

At last Sarah opened her eyes and smiled in recognition. "It looks like that's that, then," she said faintly, dismissing her own life without fuss. "Only...there was something..." her voice trailed away. Flynn was motionless, his gaze fixed on her face. Sarah closed her eyes a moment then opened them and said faintly, "There was something I wanted to..."

"Yes?" Flynn said softly, "something...?"

The tired eyes were filled with anxiety. "Everything's all right, isn't it?" she whispered. "All these years... it's been all right?"

Instinctively Toni knew Sarah was asking for the reassurance that the deception which meant so much to her had succeeded. She looked down at Flynn, wanting to weep for him. The silence seemed to stretch for an eternity while the plea in Sarah's eyes became more urgent.

Flynn shifted beside Toni and caught her fingers in a painful grip. He didn't look at her but the terrible pressure told her of his agony. She covered his hand with hers and stayed like that, willing strength and comfort to pass from her to him.

At last he spoke, his voice full of warmth and reassurance. "Of course, it's all right. It always has been."

Toni felt the tears begin to run down her cheeks at the finest performance Flynn Rawley had ever given. It convinced Sarah, for she sighed contentedly and closed her eyes. An hour later, she died.

Ten

It was early evening when they arrived at the London airport, and they drove straight to Flynn's apartment. When he saw her remove her luggage from the taxi he smiled briefly, but said nothing as they went up in the elevator together. Since Sarah's death he'd been like a man in shock. Toni had stood beside him at the grave, her heart aching at the sight of his pale, anguished face. They hadn't spoken of much except practical details, but sometimes she'd glanced up to find him watching her. He always looked hastily away, and she couldn't read his mind.

The phone was already ringing as they went in. Flynn answered and immediately his face tightened. Toni heard him growl, "I've got nothing to say. Goodbye."

"Press?" she queried.

"Yes. Putting the tickets in your name held them off for a while, but it couldn't last. I'm surprised this didn't happen before. I had nightmares about them turning up at the funeral."

"They thought you were still in London," Toni said. "I had a talk with Shep just before we left, and he promised to make sure nothing leaked out. As far as anyone could see, rehearsals have gone on as normal."

"You arranged all that?"

"Shep arranged it, and everyone in the company conspired to protect you. You've got some good friends, Flynn."

He looked at her. "Better than I knew," he said quietly.

Before she could answer, the phone rang again and she snatched it up to deal politely but firmly with another journalist. When she'd finished she fixed Flynn a large whiskey and pushed it into his hand. "I'm going to make you some supper," she said, adding quickly, "and don't tell me you can't eat."

"I wouldn't dare." He managed the ghost of a smile. "I'll do whatever the boss says. It's good that one of us can think clearly."

She kissed him and vanished into the kitchen to make him a light meal. Almost at once there was another phone call. She answered it, ready to be firm again, but the caller was an old friend of Flynn's and she handed over the receiver.

While they were eating she dealt with two more calls. Both were from journalists and she answered them shortly because they'd raised questions she wasn't ready to face. She kept her back to Flynn and she couldn't tell how much he heard. After the second call she left the receiver off.

Flynn ate mechanically and to Toni's relief some color began to come back into his cheeks. When he'd finished he poured himself another large whiskey, tossed it off, then poured another. He caught her glancing at him and raised an eyebrow. "Well?"

"Nothing. Perhaps it'll make you sleep." She knew he hadn't slept for the two nights they'd spent in Sarah's cottage, because she'd heard him pacing restlessly on the other side of the thin wall. Once she'd risen and gone to his door, but had halted there, knowing that the first move had to come from Flynn. She'd tried to argue the doubt away. After the physical closeness they'd found again at Kelby, why shouldn't she simply take him in her arms? But the barrier wouldn't be dispelled, and she knew she must wait for him to seek her if he wanted her.

She'd ventured to knock and call out to him, asking if he was all right. He'd called back that he was fine, but he hadn't opened the door. After a long time she'd gone back to her room and lain awake listening to him moving about again.

While she was busy in the kitchen Flynn came and stood in the doorway. He looked embarrassed. "It's asking a lot when you've done so much for me," he said, "but could you bear to stay here tonight?" He smiled, looking briefly like his old self. "Just as a friend?"

It hurt that he should apologize for asking for her help, as though she were a distant acquaintance with whom he had to mind his manners. "I was going to stay anyway," she said, smiling.

"You can have the bed. I'll sleep on the sofa."

"No, I'll sleep on the sofa. The phone's in here and I want to put it back on the hook, in case anyone important calls."

"Thanks. In that case I think I'll go straight to bed."

Flynn's sofa was large and comfortable but, as she'd expected, she couldn't sleep. She lay staring into the dark for an hour until the phone rang again. It was Martin Harris, from the *Daily Record*.

Toni relaxed, recognizing a man she knew slightly and liked. "Hello, Martin."

"Toni? I didn't expect to hear your voice. Are you and Flynn . . . ?"

"We're just good friends. I'm also his director, and I'm keeping a friendly eye on him."

"Can I talk to him?"

"No," she said, a little more forcefully than she'd intended.

"All right, let's talk about the show. What's happening there? Opening night's two days away and your leading man has just suffered a personal tragedy. How's he coping?"

"Very well. Flynn's a trouper. He's been through bad times before without it affecting his performance."

"You reckon to open on time then?"

Toni clenched her hand on the receiver as Harris came to the question they'd all asked. "I've made no plans to put it off," she said cautiously.

"I suppose you're waiting to see how he is at rehearsal tomorrow?"

"I have no plans to postpone the opening," Toni repeated firmly.

They dueled for a few more minutes, but at last Harris recognized defeat and hung up. Toni sighed and got to her feet. But she stopped at the sight of Flynn standing in his bedroom doorway. He was wearing pajamas and his hair was tousled. "That was Martin Harris," she said. "Don't worry, he's not as bad as some."

He came into the room. "Perhaps it's about time I started to worry instead of leaving it all to you."

"Worrying's the director's job, not the leading man's."

"Yes, I heard you on the phone. What would I have done without my friendly director to keep an eye on me? What would I have done without you, from first to last, Toni?"

She went to him. "What would *I* have done without *you* that night you let me talk out my problems?" she asked. "What would I have done without you at Kelby? Friends don't have to do without each other, and I'm the best friend you have." She said this deliberately to let him know that he could take comfort from her without fearing that she'd try to read more into it than he meant. At this moment Flynn needed uncomplicated friendship, and she loved him enough to give it to him.

"My best friend," he echoed huskily. "Thank God you are!" He put his arms around her and she drew his head down to her shoulders.

Flynn held her against him for a long time, despising himself. He'd lain awake, wondering if she'd come to him, but she hadn't, and he'd know in his heart that it was a vain hope. She'd have come to him in Ireland, if at all. The night after Sarah's death was still vivid in his mind. He'd heard Toni's footsteps outside his door, and then a long silence while he waited, his heart beating in painful anxiety, for her to turn the handle and come inside, into his arms. He'd remember all his life how it had felt to sit there as the seconds lengthened into minutes. At last she'd knocked politely on his door like a stranger and called out to him in a voice full of comradely concern. From somewhere, he'd found the pride to call back that he was fine.

But tonight, need was stronger than pride. He'd heard the phone and seized the excuse to come out and talk to her. Just to talk—that was what he'd told himself he wanted. But as he held her body next to his he knew he couldn't bear to let her go.

"Toni," he whispered against her hair, "Toni..."

At Kelby she'd worn a perfume of wicked seductiveness, but the scent in his nostrils now was her own. It was the scent of warmth and sweetness, as fresh and wholesome as she was herself. It whispered to him of earth and flowers after rain, of comfort and safety, of fires driving out the cold—all the good things of the world. It invaded him through all his senses, overcoming grief and despair.

She raised her face and he felt her lips soft against his. His kiss was tentative until her lips parted to welcome him, and then his tongue sought its home in the moist darkness of her mouth. The tension that had possessed his body melted away, and he felt his flesh become alive again. He'd thought that weariness must have killed all desire in him, but now he found he was wrong.

Toni, her body pressed intimately to his, felt the manifestation of his need, and let him know, with tender caresses, that she wanted him. Through the thin silk of his pajamas she could trace the outlines of the hard, masculine frame, the long spine leading down to the narrow hips and firm buttocks. Her hands lingered, relishing his muscular form, before moving around to seek out his maleness. She encompassed it with gentle fingers and he groaned aloud. "Toni," he said raggedly.

"Come with me," she whispered, taking him by the hand and leading him back into the bedroom.

At Kelby they'd seduced each other lightheartedly, enjoying a passion spiced with laughter. Now she knew he needed something different. Instead of a teasing play of undressing slowly, she pulled off her nightgown in one movement. He followed her lead, stripping off the pajamas and opening his arms to enfold her nakedness against his own. She drew him down onto the bed, where the warmth of their bodies mingled in a wordless giving and receiving that was the sweetest they'd ever shared. He sought her at once and she invited him lovingly into herself, holding him in an embrace of passionate tenderness till their moment came. She was his in any way he wanted her—wife, lover or friend, whatever would ease his sadness.

For Flynn it was as though a wound had been healed. Toni's warmth enveloped him, making the ground steady again beneath his feet. Afterward, as he lay in her arms, his head against her breast, he found he could talk freely for the first time since Sarah's death. "For years I've tried not to look too deeply inside myself, in case there was a hollow place there, where *I* should be. I guess now I'll have to find a way of coming to terms with it."

"But there isn't a hollow place," Toni said. "There's a man in there that you've created yourself. Flynn Rawley is a great actor."

"That's another way of saying an illusionist, but there has to be something behind the illusion. Now I'll never know."

"Flynn," she said urgently, "you couldn't have done anything else. The kindest thing you ever did was to tell your mother what she wanted to hear. It meant so much to her to think she'd kept her secret."

"I know you're right. I'm glad now. I didn't think I could get the words out, and if you hadn't been there I'm not sure I could have done it."

"You would, I know you would, because you loved her."

Flynn hesitated a moment before saying, "You've always had a false picture of me, Toni. You've always thought I was stronger and better than I was. But the strength came from you. I've wondered sometimes why you couldn't see that, it was so obvious."

"It wasn't obvious to me, but then, I was little more than a child when we married," she said, tentatively feeling her way to understanding. "You were the knight in shining armor who rescued me from Farrowdale, and I worshiped you. I was too young to see how that hero worship can be a burden on the hero."

"Don't blame yourself for being young. I was young, too, or I might have realized that there were things you needed that I wasn't giving you. You needed them so badly that you had to leave me to find them. You wouldn't have made such a success of your life if we'd stayed together."

A success of her life? Toni savored the phrase and found it bitter.

"This is hindsight talking," Flynn went on. "I can see now why you were better away from me, but at the time I came close to hating you. I felt as though the earth had shaken under me and for a while I nearly cracked up."

"You?" she said, amazed.

"Yes," he said wryly. "Me. Things never came as easily to me as you thought, but I coped all right when you were there. Then suddenly you weren't and...well, anyway, now you know the truth. I'm not a knight in shining armor. I'm not sure what I am. All I know is that we're almost at opening night and I'm so confused that I'm no use to myself or anyone else."

Toni heard the note of desperation in his voice. Her own words came back to her: *You see the other person unhappy...that's when real love starts to hurt.* She loved this man with a love more real than anything else on earth, and it hurt. She stared into the darkness, taking a moment to brace herself against the pain of what she was about to do, before saying calmly, "Then we'll postpone the opening."

Flynn made a violent movement, pulling himself out of her arms and looking down at her. "What did you say?" he demanded quietly.

"We'll postpone the opening. Everyone will understand. We'll open when you feel up to it."

"But what about Greg Benskin? He'll go back to New York and that'll be the end of your Broadway chance."

"Not necessarily. I dare say he'll come back." She smiled and tried to sound convincing, but she knew her words were meaningless. She could wait years for this moment to come again. But she'd counted the cost before she made her offer, and she knew Flynn was worth it.

He drew back farther and looked down to where he could just make her out in the dim light. "You'd really do that for me?" he asked in wonder.

"Of course I would. I'll call Shep in the morning."

Flynn got up from the bed and went to stand at the window, staring out but not seeing the view. He was looking at the pale face of a disillusioned young woman, at the stains of the tears he'd brought her, hearing her cry, "I'm tired of clinging to the great Flynn Rawley's coattails. I'm tired of suffocating in your clouds of glory. I want some glory of my own."

Since their parting he'd watched her fighting her way up the slippery pole, longing to reach out a hand to help her, but knowing that any help from him would be bitterly rejected. She'd protected her independence fiercely until now she was almost at the top. One final leap would make her totally free of him, and he knew what that freedom meant to her. Yet she'd offered the sacrifice for his sake.

"No." His voice was suddenly firm again as he turned in to the room. "I told you once that you don't get to the very top by throwing away your chances. It's still true. We'll open when we said we would. This is your golden moment, Toni. I'm not going to be the reason it passed you by."

She scrambled out of bed. "But Flynn, think what it means. Two days . . . you can't . . ."

"Yes I can." For a moment she heard the old Flynn, the one who knew he could do anything, whose dazzling accomplishments had often made her feel useless. But she knew better now. He'd removed the mask to let her glimpse the vulnerable man beneath, and though he might replace it she could never be fooled again.

"I can," he repeated. "But you'll have to help me. Stay with me, and let me hold on to you—" he drew her close "—just for a little longer."

Eleven

On opening night Toni arrived at the theater two hours ahead of curtain time. Shep was there and whistled at her elegant dark-blue velvet pantsuit, but he looked surprised to see her alone. "Flynn will be along in an hour," she said.

"How is he?"

"In a black depression, but that's normal. He's always suffered from stage fright. It gets more intense as opening night nears, and on the last afternoon he's impossible to live with. I think it's worse this time, but it's hard to tell because he's so quiet."

They wandered into the auditorium, where the curtain was up, showing an army of stagehands setting up the scenery for the first act. It looked garish and flat now, but when it was properly lit it would be a magical evocation of a medieval Italian palace, drenched in sunlight and touched by soft sea breezes.

Toni's gaze moved upward to the red plush and gold of the dress circle and gallery. In two hours those seats would be filled with people ready to pass judgment on Toni Locksley and Flynn Rawley. The story of Sarah's death had appeared in the papers although, to Toni's relief, no journalist had discovered the other story behind it. Flynn's decision that "the show must go on" had brought him some popular acclaim, but Toni knew that the same people who praised him would be watching him like hawks tonight, ready to damn him if he disappointed them.

"I'm glad you two have gotten back together," Shep was saying. "Who'd have thought an old sinner like me could play Cupid?"

"Shep, it's not like that," Toni said quickly. "I'm just staying with Flynn for a few days to help him over the worst. As soon as this is over I'll be moving out."

"But that's crazy. You two belong together."

"It looks that way now," Toni conceded hesitantly. "But it's like everything else in the theater, an illusion. You know how emotional people get when they're doing a play? They swear lifelong friendship, or love, then the play breaks up and suddenly all the feeling's gone."

"And you think what's happening to you and Flynn is no more than that? C'mon, Toni."

"I've been in this game too long to be fooled by an illusion. If this is a success I'll be doing something else soon, and then Flynn and I won't even meet anymore." She smiled. "We won't need each other then."

Shep looked skeptical but said, "I suppose you know your own business best, but it's a shame when you've done so much for each other. I can tell you now that when the clamor for your services starts I expect to have first option—after Greg Benskin, of course."

"Is he definitely coming?" Toni asked eagerly.

"I'll be leaving to collect him in a few minutes." Shep shook his head at her in wonder. "To think of the fight I had to make you do this show."

"I never did say yes, you know. I told Flynn I refused, definitely and finally, and he just didn't seem to hear."

Shep grinned. "That's his way, isn't it? Underneath those mild manners Flynn has a good deal of ruthlessness. He disguises it with charm and laughter, so that half the time you don't realize what's really going on. But when your head's stopped spinning you'll find that what's happened, *every time*, is what suits Flynn Rawley."

"Shep," she protested, "I thought you liked Flynn."

"Sure, I like him, especially when I consider how much money he's going to make for me. No, seriously, I'm very fond of Flynn, but I know that the only thing that distinguishes him from some of the other smart operators in this business is that he'll be courteous while he's taking you for a ride. Manipulation's his middle name, Toni, you've always know that. You as good as warned me about it when you were saying you couldn't work with him."

"Did I?" she asked vaguely. "I can't remember what I said, it seems so long ago."

"Well, I must be going," Shep said, kissing her. "All the luck in the world, dear, but I have no doubts."

"Thanks, Shep."

He departed and Toni went backstage. There was nothing more she could do to the production, and her only duty now was to put heart into the cast. She'd written personal notes of thanks and encouragement to the leading players and now she went around putting them in place in the dressing rooms. When she'd finished she went to Flynn's room because her note to him still hadn't been written. She'd made five attempts and torn up every one.

He hadn't arrived yet and she sat down at his dressing table to try once more to put into words everything she wanted to say to him. But she stopped almost at once, because she couldn't speak her true thoughts: I love you, and I want to come back to you and be your wife forever. I've understood the truth at last. Please tell me it's not too late.

She couldn't say these things because to put emotional pressure on Flynn at this moment would be unforgivable, but she also feared to say them, because she was sure he didn't feel the same. He'd gone out of his way to tell her she was better off without him, and although he'd asked her to stay, he'd stressed that it was "just for a little longer."

After tonight they'd go their separate ways and the success of the show would be a goodbye present from each to the other. The thought of losing him finally, after drawing so close to him again, spread a chill over her heart.

There was another chill, too, that she didn't want to face. Shep's words came back to her: " . . . a good deal of ruthlessness...what happens *every time* is what suits Flynn Rawley."

Flynn had once said the same: "I'll do anything to get the best out of myself, and I let *nothing* stand in the way of that best. I'm never kind where my work's concerned. . . ."

Everything that had happened between them could be explained like that, she realized. Even the way he'd devoted himself to her at Kelby might be no more than the astuteness of an actor who knew he needed his director in good shape. She passed a hand over her eyes, trying to drive the dreadful thought away.

From below came the sound of squealing fans. Toni went to the window that overlooked the stage door, and saw that Flynn had just arrived. Hastily she seized the pen and scribbled:

Dear Flynn,
But for you, none of this would be happening. Bless you for making me do it. I trusted you, and I wasn't wrong. Now you must trust me, and have as much faith in yourself as I have in you.

Toni

She put it quickly in an envelope and left it propped against the mirror. She wasn't a moment too soon, because almost immediately Flynn appeared. There was a suppressed tension in his manner and his eyes were dark, but he smiled at her. "Well, I made it as far as the theater, and that's the first hurdle dealt with," he quipped. "I can't tell you how tempted I was to put my head under the pillow and hope everything would go away."

"You cleared the second hurdle, too," Toni responded, matching his tone with a light one of her own. "I was afraid the hordes downstairs would devour you."

Flynn struck an attitude. "Sensational debut of understudy after leading man eaten alive," he intoned. "Fan declares, 'He tasted of sardines.' Last night mourning theatrical colleagues said, 'He was always a fishy character.'" He caught a glimpse of her expression and said, "Sorry, it's my night for rotten jokes."

"I'll forgive you," Toni said, laughing. "It wasn't a bad effort under the circumstances."

There was a knock on the door and the stage manager put his head around. "Toni, we've got a small crisis—"

She gave Flynn's shoulder a quick squeeze and departed to deal with the drama that was disrupting preparations in the chorus girls' dressing room. She felt more peace of mind than before. Whatever strain he was under, Flynn was bearing up well.

She made the rounds to the other leading players, cheering them up, dispelling nerves as far as she could, but the atmosphere of tension was almost tangible now. Through the curtains they could all hear the sounds of the auditorium beginning to fill up. A few members of the orchestra were in place, tuning up with small, tantalizing snatches of music. Duff appeared, magnificent in tails, ready to take his place as conductor. *"Nos morituri te salutamus,"* he murmured, glassy eyed.

"I salute you, too," Toni said with a chuckle, "but neither of us is about to die."

"I'm half dead with fright already," he said, and passed on.

Toni felt a touch on her arm and turned to see Harvey, Flynn's elderly dresser, his face anxious. "Can you come?" he asked urgently.

She was at Flynn's room in a moment. He was half dressed in tights and a flowing shirt. He sat with one arm leaning on his dressing table, taking deep, painful breaths. Harvey closed the door and left them alone. Toni dropped to her knees beside Flynn, with that helpless feeling of being in a strange country. In the past she'd watched his stage fright building up for days beforehand, but he'd seldom allowed her into his dressing room on an opening night and she'd never seen him like this before. "Flynn . . ." she said.

He looked at her out of desperate eyes. "Toni, I can't remember anything. None of the lines, none of the moves, *anything*. It's all gone clean out of my head."

Toni looked at him for a moment, then crossed her fingers. She was going to take a huge risk but it had to be done. If Flynn suspected she was worried, too, he'd have nothing to hold on to.

"It doesn't matter," she said. She got to her feet and looked at his face in the mirror. "You'd better finish putting your makeup on," she said.

"Toni, didn't you hear what I said? I can't remember a damn thing. It's as though I'd never read the script."

"Yes, I heard you. Turn your head a little so that I can finish your eyes."

"You seem remarkably cool about this."

"Well, it's nonsense, isn't it?" she said with a slight shrug. "You know it'll all come back when you hear yourself saying the first line. You taught me a trick once for dealing with it. Check your first line just before you make your entrance, and then stop worrying."

Out of the corner of her eye she could see that her unruffled manner was having its effect. Flynn was calming down visibly.

"Ten minutes, please," came the voice over the loud speaker. Quickly she helped him finish dressing and stood back to regard him.

Flynn had vanished. In his place was Benedick, a swaggering young man, lusty with life, whose ribald, anarchic smile was an invitation to the ladies and a challenge to the men.

"Overture and beginners, please!"

Toni saw Flynn pale beneath his makeup. She took his hands quickly. "It's all right," she said.

"If I get the words in the right order and don't trip over the scenery, that's as much as I think we can ask," he said wryly.

"That's as much as I'm expecting," she assured him. "I knew it was a risk when I took you on, but I said to myself, 'He's got no talent but he tries hard, and he comes cheap.'"

His wrathful eyes met hers for a moment, then his lips twitched and he murmured, "To hell with you, Toni Locksley."

Before she could reply he'd swept her into a bear hug that almost crushed the life out of her, and then he was gone.

Over the loudspeaker she heard the stage manager mutter, "House lights," followed by a sudden hush from the audience, a burst of applause as Duff appeared, then total silence. Toni stayed where she was, listening as the orchestra crashed into the opening bars of the overture. It was vivid, up-tempo music, which got the evening away to a sparkling start. But soon the mood changed with the first love song, a beautiful tune full of yearning regret for the past, and Toni felt something catch in her throat. She'd heard it many times, but never before had it seemed to speak to her as it did tonight. The words "too late" sighed hauntingly through each bar, and she found that her eyes had blurred.

She pulled herself together sharply and left the room, arriving in the wings just as the overture was finishing to generous applause. The curtain went up, and the chorus swirled into the first number. She could see Flynn standing apart in his own pool of silence, apparently oblivious of his cue growing nearer.

But when the cue came he started into life to make his entrance with a crowd of laughing companions. He managed his first line without hesitation, although there was a slight tremor in his voice. Toni held her breath, but after a few more lines he got his first laugh and she began to relax.

Beatrice and Benedick had a witty exchange that went well, and so did the duet that followed in which they continued bickering to music.

The highlight of the evening was the masked ball, with its magical effect of swirling blue and silver drapes. Beatrice and Benedick danced, challenging each other from behind the protection of their masks. Then the scene froze, and the lights changed to an otherworldly glow. Slowly they lowered their masks and looked at each other, man and woman, recognizing the truth too late. The haunting strains of the love song filled the theater, their voices combining in an expression of poignant regret. He took her in his arms for a long kiss while a solo violin echoed the theme. Then they drew apart, resumed their former positions and hid themselves again behind masks. It had all been a dream.

When the scene ended there was thunderous applause, which brought balm to Toni's heart—she'd worked on that effect until it was the cornerstone of the evening. If it had gotten through to the audience the whole show was alive, and everyone else knew it had.

Toni became aware that people were beginning to look at her differently, but didn't realize that it was because she'd acquired the aura of success.

Now the mood onstage changed to one of riotous comedy as Benedick's friends conspired to make him believe Beatrice was half dead with love for him. Toni had placed Flynn so that the audience could see his face as he overheard the conversation, knowing that his genius for comic dumb show would do the rest. She was right. Without saying a word Flynn had the audience in fits. Toni rejoiced for him because she knew that an audience's laughter was his lifeblood. But she also rejoiced for herself, because now she could see that the miracle was happening—the miracle she and Flynn had wrought together.

The friends launched into a lively trio, "Benedick, the Married Man," and danced offstage to loud applause. Benedick emerged, his face baffled as he remarked, "They seem to pit the lady," and the audience rocked at his discomfiture, but the next moment he'd quelled them to silence with the awed question, "Love *me*?"

Standing onstage alone, Flynn dominated the huge theater with total mastery. He talked to the audience as though they were friends he'd invited for the evening, producing arguments this way and that, seizing on their slightest reaction and making his next line seem to grow from it. He had them in the palm of his hand, and they adored him.

"That's a real love affair you're witnessing," George muttered in Toni's ear. "Flynn Rawley and his audience. Neither of them needs anyone else."

"I'm afraid you're right," Toni said sadly.

Now he was singing a witty song that built up to the triumphant cry, "I will be horribly in love with her." The curtain came down on the first half, the audience broke into a deafening roar, and Flynn came offstage. He met Toni's eyes just once and then they were both submerged by the excited cast. Toni understood that look. Something had changed between them forever. It had started when she'd offered to sacrifice her Broadway hopes for his sake, and now the circle was being completed as he pushed himself to the limit for her. Tonight's success was something they'd given to each other, and it had made them equals at last.

In the second half, tragedy took over the story. Beatrice's cousin was slandered, her wedding brutally broken off at the altar. As Beatrice wept alone in the church afterward, Benedick tried to console her. "I do love nothing in the world so well as you," he told her softly. "Is not that strange?"

Toni's heart missed a beat at the note of wondrous revelation in Flynn's voice, and the subtle skill with which he showed a man at the moment when love ceases to be merry and becomes deep and painful.

The story moved to its climax. The tragedy was swept away, Beatrice and Benedick rediscovered their love and the curtain fell on a triumphant finale. The bellow from the audience told everyone what they wanted to know.

The cast bowed again and again but the applause went on with no end in sight. Flynn and Carole bowed together, then Flynn stepped forward alone and the cheers became a roar. Toni stood in the wings and watched him through eyes blurred with tears.

Flowers were pouring down onto the stage, piling up around his feet. Flynn scooped some up and gave them to Carole, then headed toward the wings. Before Toni knew what he meant to do he'd seized her hand and was pulling her onto the stage. The cheers grew louder at the sight of her, then louder again as Flynn scooped up some more flowers and presented them to her.

She stood there stunned, trying to take in what was happening to her, while the sound crashed around her like waves. She looked at Flynn, leading the applause for her, and tried to see his eyes, but he was wearing a brilliant professional smile that covered his face like a mask.

Twelve

Half an hour after the curtain fell the stage was set up for a party, with trestle tables loaded with food and drink. The mood was exuberant, with everyone high on hope.

Shep arrived with a large grey-haired man with sharp eyes, whom he introduced as Greg Benskin. Benskin shook Toni's hand and studied her closely. "I'm sorry I can't stay around longer to join the celebration," he said, "because you people really have something to celebrate. But you and I will be seeing plenty more of each other, Miss Locksley. My congratulations."

He gave her a brief nod and departed. Shep went with him, pausing just long enough to give Toni a smile and a thumbs-up sign. She stood looking after the two men while the others milled around her, voicing their congratulations. She never heard them. Her eyes were searching out Flynn, who appeared by her side suddenly with a glass of champagne that he thrust into her hand. "Make the most of her now, folks," he caroled, "because after tonight it'll be sixpence to talk to her."

It was Flynn who toasted her and led the singing of "For she's a jolly good fellow," but it seemed to Toni that he was avoiding her eye. He was still nervous about something, and she thought she could guess what it was. Flynn hated hurting people, and he wasn't looking forward to telling her that they'd come to the parting of the ways. He'd worked to give her a big success so that he could leave her with an easy conscience. She watched him being the life and soul of the party, always managing to stay out of her range, and her conviction grew.

In the early hours a lull fell over the crowd and they looked at each other with fearful eyes. It was easy to assure themselves that the show must surely be a smash, but the critics' verdict was the one that mattered. George went out to search for the early editions, and reappeared, laden with papers that were snatched off him and hastily riffled through.

The first squeal of delight went up, then another and another. More champagne was opened. People surrounded Toni, kissing and pummeling her. She tried to catch Flynn's eye. She'd have loved to share this moment with him alone, to read together the notice that started, "Mask or face—director's brilliant conception," and went on, "Last night the Rawleys, husband and wife, did the town proud...." His own notices were an actor's dream, "Performance of a lifetime...a master of every mood..." But rave reviews were no new experience for him; it would have been nice to ask him how he'd felt the first time, and compare notes.

But Flynn, too, was the center of an excited group and seemed to have forgotten all about her. Toni forced herself to make the proper responses to everyone around her, but she was suddenly very tired.

"I think I'll go home now," she said as soon as she decently could, "and the rest of you should do the same. The second night's got to be even better."

She said her goodbyes, but when she got to Duff she stopped and looked about her at the thinning party. "Where's Flynn?" she said.

"He left several minutes ago," Duff said. "But he asked me to give you this." He held out an envelope.

Toni thrust the note into her pocket and didn't take it out until she was in the corridor. She could hardly believe Flynn had done this—taken what he wanted, left without a word or a smile to her, and trusted his explanations to a letter. Bitterly she pulled open the envelope, but as she read the contents she grew very still.

Darling Toni,

I never doubted that this moment would come, because you're a brilliant director, with or without me. But you had to find out for yourself before I could say the things I wanted to. I've spent hours planning the right phrases, and now they've all left my head completely. But perhaps if I just tell you that Liz Watkins never existed, you'll understand.

Love, Flynn

Toni stared at the words, trying to understand them. Three years ago Flynn had asked her to stay married to him to save him from Liz Watkins' clutches, but Liz had never existed. So why—?

Toni began to run as if her life depended on it. In the street she hailed a cab and gave him Flynn's address. As they drew up outside the apartment building she was sure she saw a curtain move in Flynn's window. All the way up in the elevator her heart was pounding with terrified hope. The first thing she saw when she ran out of the elevator was his open front door, and in another moment she was enfolded in his arms, with his mouth crushing hers.

"Why?" she demanded as soon as she could speak. "Flynn, *why*?"

"I never meant to divorce you," he said simply. "Not for one moment." He bent his head and there was another long silence, but he retained sufficient presence of mind to kick the door shut and draw her farther into the room and down onto the sofa. At last he released her, but he kept his arms around her as though afraid to let her go.

"Sweet, darling Toni, we belong together, and we always will. Tell me you feel that, too."

"Yes...yes..." she told him between kisses. "But—"

"But we married too young. If I'd been older I might have known how not to suffocate you. If you'd been older you might have known how to stand up to my success without leaving me. When you left it half killed me, but I knew my only chance was to keep quiet while you found your feet.

"I did some wheeling and dealing to keep you legally mine. I invented Liz Watkins, and then I managed to be elusive whenever you mentioned divorce. I was biding my time, waiting for the moment when I could beg you to come back to me. But I knew it had to be exactly the *right* moment, when you were strong and successful and felt you'd emerged from my shadow.

"When Shep asked you to do the show I thought my chance had come. But then you told me about Alec Wrighton and that scared me to death. I've been half mad with jealousy and treading on eggshells in case I did the wrong thing. That night we talked about Beatrice and Benedick I was sending you coded messages, but you didn't seem to understand."

"You *were* talking about us," she said breathlessly. "I wondered, but I didn't dare believe it. I thought you'd gotten carried away by the characters."

"I did, but only because they were so like us. Couldn't you hear what I was really trying to say? When you froze I thought it must be because of Wrighton, and I made up my mind to meet him and see what I was up against; I knew I had to act quickly. I was determined to get you into my bed, by hook or by crook."

"And knowing you, it would be 'by crook,'" she said, smiling shakily.

"Well, Shep warned you tonight what an unscrupulous character I am—he told me during the intermission. It's true. I've been stringing you along since the day you walked out, pretending to be 'just friendly,' and all the time waiting for the perfect time to lure you into my trap." He grinned. "If you want a divorce now, I can make you wait another five years." But then the laughter died abruptly, "I don't mean that. I won't hold you against your will."

"You said I was better off without you," she reminded him.

"Yes, you are. Especially now. I watched you tonight. You were so much in your element that I had to go away and not see any more. You don't need me. It's me that needs you. You can't imagine what a temptation it was to let you put off the opening until after Benskin had left, but if you'd done that I couldn't have looked you in the eye again. You can only love me in freedom, not if I'm a millstone around your neck."

"Shall I tell you what you are?" she said softly. "Flynn Rawley is the man I love. He always has been, and he always will be."

"It was when you made me that offer I began to hope you really did love me." He looked into her face for a long moment as if trying to read her soul. Then he took her hands and kissed the palms, first one, then the other. "Stay with me, Toni. I love you so, and if I'm not the man you love, I'm not anything."

"What about tonight? Isn't Flynn Rawley, the star, 'anything'?"

"Flynn Rawley, the star, is a shadow that ceases to exist when the audience goes home. I don't need an audience, I need *you*." He took her face between his hands. "I do love nothing in the world so well as you," he said huskily. "But it isn't strange. Nothing could be more natural than to love you. I made a mess of it the first time—"

"*We* made a mess of it," she corrected him lovingly.

"All right, 'we.' But thank God, life does sometimes give you second chances."

Searching his eyes she found what she'd longed to see. The mask was gone now. There remained only the man, open and defenseless, and glad to be so because he loved her and trusted her love. She surrendered herself to his kiss, as confidently happy now as she'd been that first time, ten years ago. But she knew also that the years had changed them, allowing them to grow until they reached the place where they could love as equals. This time there'd be no parting.

* * * * *